The RETURN *of* GABRIEL

ALSO BY JOHN ARMISTEAD

The $66 Summer

For my grandsons,
Will and Ethan

With special appreciation to Lloyd Gray Jr., Callie Smith, Lena Mitchell, and Danny McKenzie for reading over the manuscript and making suggestions, and to my literary agent, Evelyn Singer, for wise counsel and helpful advice through every phase of the writing of this book, and to Sandi, William, Audra, Charlotte, David, and Laura for their love and support.

The
RETURN
of
GABRIEL

JOHN ARMISTEAD

ILLUSTRATIONS BY FRAN GREGORY

MILKWEED
EDITIONS

The characters and events in this book are fictitious. Any similarity to real persons, living or dead, is coincidental and not intended by the author.

Published 2002 by Milkweed Editions
Printed in the United States of America
Cover and interior design by Dale Cooney
Cover and interior art by Fran Gregory
Author photo by David Armistead
The text of this book is set in Plantin.
02 03 04 05 06   5 4 3 2 1
First Edition

Special underwriting for this book was provided by the James R. Thorpe Foundation.

Milkweed Editions, a nonprofit publisher, gratefully acknowledges support for our intermediate fiction from Alliance for Reading funders: Marshall Field's Project Imagine with support from the Target Foundation; Target Stores; United Arts Partnership Funds; and West Group. Other support has been provided by Bush Foundation; General Mills Foundation; McKnight Foundation; Minnesota State Arts Board through an appropriation by the Minnesota State Legislature and a grant from the National Endowment for the Arts, and a grant from the Wells Fargo Foundation Minnesota; A Resource for Change technology grant from the National Endowment for the Arts; St. Paul Companies, Inc.; and generous individuals.

Library of Congress Cataloging-in-Publication Data

Armistead, John.
    The return of Gabriel / John Armistead.
       p. cm.
       Summary: In the summer of 1964, a thirteen-year-old white boy whose best friend is black is caught in the middle when civil rights workers and Ku Klux Klan members clash in a small town near Tupelo, Mississippi.
       ISBN 1-57131-637-X (alk. paper)—ISBN 1-57131-638-8 (pbk. : alk. paper)
       1. African Americans—Juvenile fiction.   [1. African Americans—Fiction.
2. Friendship—Fiction.   3. Civil rights movements—Fiction.   4. Race relations—Fiction.   5. Mississippi—History—20th century—Fiction.   6. United States—History—1961–1969—Fiction.]   I. Title.
       PZ7.A728 Re 2002
       [Fic]—dc21

                                                                  2002002796

This book is printed on acid-free paper.

The
RETURN
of
GABRIEL

ONE

JUBAL MADE A FACE when I first said we ought to let Squirrel Kogan join the Scorpions, but I quickly reminded him Squirrel's father had a big stack of lumber in their backyard.

I mentioned it when Jubal and I were clearing undergrowth from the site we'd selected to build the hideout. It was on the western edge of my family's land on a bluff overlooking the creek and very close to the falling-down barbed wire fence that marked the property line. On the other side of the fence was Mr. Gideon Montgomery's land. The vines and brambles of the forest had swallowed up most of the fence.

"Cooper, you exasperate me," Jubal said. "Just how many peoples we gonna let in this club anyways?"

"Since right now it's just you and me, I figure one more ain't going to crowd us much," I said. "And we gonna need some strong walls if Reno McCarthy attacks."

Jubal halted his machete in midswing. I knew that would get his attention.

Reno lived a couple miles down the road. He was forever coming up to me at school and saying something like, "You want a part of me?" I wouldn't answer him and he'd laugh and make sounds like a chicken. I didn't know anybody in the world I disliked more than Reno McCarthy. Jubal felt the same way, but for different reasons.

It was people like Reno who were all the time picking on other people for no good reason that got me to thinking about forming the Scorpions. The Scorpions would be "One for all, and all for one." That was our motto, and if somebody attacked one of us, all the rest would rush to his defense.

"Reno ain't studying us," said Jubal.

He brought the machete down hard, ripping clean through the trunk of the sapling and burying the blade into the dirt. He attacked several more in a fury. Small trees fell left and right. I went along behind, pulling the trees to the edge of the hillside. The mention of Reno never failed to get a response.

Jubal and I were both thirteen that summer of 1964, but he was half a head taller than me and thirty pounds heavier. Of course, he came big—twice my size when we were born, hardly a month apart—but I was determined by the time school started to gain ten pounds and be much, much stronger. Jubal and I were working out together each day that summer, running and doing weights.

Jubal had selected the site. His school, like all the colored schools in Mississippi, let out for the summer a month before ours, so he had plenty of time to roam around the woods. It would be easier to defend our position on the bluff, and it wasn't five minutes from Big Bend. Big Bend was a place where the creek turned back on itself like a water moccasin and was deep enough to swim in.

"Just how much lumber has Squirrel's daddy got anyways?" Jubal asked.

"A big pile," I said.

He stuck the machete in the dirt and wiped his face with a red handkerchief. "And another thing," he said. "How come Squirrel be going to y'all's school instead of ours?"

"I done told you," I said. "He's white. That's how come."

Jubal jutted his jaw. "Reverend Graham say Jews are colored."

I had to admit Jubal had a point there. Our pastor, Reverend Graham, knew all about the Bible and he'd mentioned in several sermons that Jesus was a Jew and, since Jesus was a person of color, Jews were colored too.

Reverend Graham based this on Revelations, which said that Jesus had hair like wool. "Now, who's got hair like wool?" he'd shout. "I'll tell you who. The Negro race, that's who."

No, I wasn't going to go against my pastor. But, to be honest, being the only white member of Oak Grove Baptist Church, I did feel a little uneasy when Reverend Graham made such a big ado over Jesus being colored, and secretly I hoped maybe I had a little colored blood in me.

Of course, with my blue eyes and light brown hair, I knew it couldn't be more than a drop or two, but I'd seen coloreds as light as me.

Jubal was insistent. "So? Is he passing or what?"

"I think Jews must have faded a lot since Bible times," I said. "After all, that was before George Washington even."

We threw the saplings and brush down the hillside toward the fence and walked back to the road, where I'd parked my motor scooter.

My scooter was a Cushman Highlander that I bought secondhand last year with forty-six dollars Uncle Chicago loaned me. I needed one since I'd gotten a paper route with the *Tupelo Daily Journal.* I had eighty-three customers spread out all over the western side of Chulosa.

"At least his hair's curlier than yours," Jubal said.

I didn't reply.

TWO

SQUIRREL KOGAN lived across the highway from our farm. Squirrel was hands down the smartest boy in our class at school but did his best to hide it. He was always getting in trouble with the teacher for making wisecracks that made the whole class laugh. "He always makes me laugh," I told Jubal. "And he knows more fart jokes than anybody in the world."

Squirrel was the only one from school I saw much of during the summer. None of my other classmates lived nearby, except for Reno, and, to be sure, I didn't have anything to do with him.

Mrs. Kogan smiled at us when she came to the back door. "You boys want some peanut butter cookies?" she asked. "I'm just taking them out of the oven." She sat us at the kitchen table and then called out, "Aaron, your friends have come to see you." She poured each of us a glass of milk.

Afterward, we talked with Squirrel in the shade of the large pecan tree in his backyard.

"Why do I have to swear anything?" he asked. "What's this all about?"

Jubal scowled at me. I gave a slight nod toward the stack of lumber by the barn. The lumber came from an old shed Mr. Kogan had pulled down.

"It's secret," I said. "Very secret. So you have to swear to die if you tell anybody."

He thought about it a moment, then said, "Okay. I swear. Now, what is it?"

"No," said Jubal, looking down at Squirrel. "You have to say it. You have to say, 'I swear to death I won't tell nobody.' That way, if you tell, God will strike you down dead."

"Do I have to use your incorrect grammar in this oath?" asked Squirrel.

"Let's go, Coop," Jubal said to me.

"Wait," I said. "It was just a joke, wasn't it, Squirrel?"

"Okay," Squirrel said with a sigh. "I swear to death I won't tell anyone." He pushed his glasses back up on his face with the back of his hand. He was all the time doing that, and the glasses would slip down to the end of his nose a minute later and he'd do it again.

I told him about the Scorpions, that it was a very secret and highly selective group.

"Who all is in it?"

"That's one of the secrets."

"What do y'all do?"

"That's secret too. But I can tell you this. It's 'One for all, and all for one.'"

"I have a question for you," said Jubal. "Was your grandmother darker than you?"

"What?" Squirrel asked. His eyes, which were already magnified behind his thick lenses, seemed to grow larger.

"Of course, you will have to go through the initiation," I said.

"What kind of initiation?"

"That's secret," I said.

"And it ain't easy," added Jubal.

Squirrel shoved his hands into his pockets and squinched up his nose. "I don't think I care to join," he said.

"Did you know Jesus was colored?" asked Jubal. His tone was challenging.

"What are you talking about?" Squirrel frowned and pushed his glasses up again.

"Listen," I said. "We're going to do some death-defying adventures."

Jubal gave me a questioning look.

I continued, "Besides, the initiation isn't really all that bad."

"It's pretty bad," said Jubal.

Now it was my turn to give him a look. He didn't know any more than I did what the initiation was. We'd never discussed it.

"I'll think about it," said Squirrel.

"We need an answer now," said Jubal.

"I'll tell you what," I said. "Let's make it real easy. Say, maybe you could just get some lumber from some-place to help with the hideout."

"What hideout?"

"That's secret."

"Come on, Coop," Jubal said to me. "Can't you see he ain't interested? Besides, we don't need no lumber from him."

I wished he would shut up and let me do the talking. "Maybe just a few pieces from that pile over there," I said.

"My father is saving that."

"I know where we can get plenty of lumber," said Jubal, walking away. "We gave him a chance. He ain't getting no second chances."

I gave Squirrel a good-bye wave and followed Jubal.

"I think I might want to join after all," Squirrel called after us.

"We'll think about it," Jubal said without looking back.

I smiled and waved again at Squirrel. "Great," I said. "We'll get back with you."

I hurried after Jubal toward my scooter, which was parked in front of the house.

"What is wrong with you?" I asked. "He was ready to get those boards for us."

"We can get some on the Montgomery place," Jubal said.

"The Montgomery place? Are you crazy? That old man will kill us if he sees us on his land."

"He ain't killed nobody in a long time," Jubal said with a grin. "Now start this thing up."

THREE

WE RODE BACK UP the red dirt road toward my uncle Chicago's house and parked beside the path leading to the hideout site. The hot sun slipped through the thick overhead branches of hardwoods and splattered the ground here and there with soft light.

"When was you ever on the Montgomery place?" I asked, knowing I'd never set foot over there myself even though their land adjoined ours.

"Daddy took me once," he said. "That's where he was raised."

Jubal rarely mentioned his father. Marcellus Harris had hanged himself in jail four years before. He was in jail for being drunk and getting into a fight. I never mentioned Marcellus to Jubal because I knew it all must be an embarrassment to him.

Glory never said anything about Marcellus either. Glory was Jubal's mother and cooked for my family every evening except on weekends. Last year she married a man named Jerome Suddith who had a house in the colored quarters, and Glory, Jubal, and his sister and brother all moved in with him.

"You sure it was the Montgomery place?" I asked, not hiding the skepticism in my voice. It was a well-known fact that old man Montgomery had killed a man with a knife once.

"It was a long time ago," said Jubal. "I was little, but I still remembers it good. Me and Daddy was rabbit hunting. Mr. Montgomery said we could hunt on his land. And Daddy showed me his old house."

"What about Ike Montgomery?" I asked, referring to Mr. Montgomery's son, who worked at Magnolia Meats with Poppa. "What's he going to think about us getting that lumber?"

"Ike ain't ever there 'cept at night, and old Mr. Montgomery never leaves the house. Nobody would ever see us." Jubal paused at the fence line separating our property from the Montgomerys'. "Besides, it ain't like we gonna steal the boards," he said.

"Then how come we don't just go ask him for them?" I said sarcastically.

"Those houses are falling down anyways. We just going to borrow enough to make the hideout. It'll save them having to haul it off or burn it up some day."

"And what if that old man sees us helping him out? He's gonna fill our butts with buckshot."

"You ain't scared, is you?" Jubal asked with a grin. "I thought the Scorpions ain't scared of nothing."

"Maybe we ought to ask Squirrel one more time.

That lumber of his daddy's is probably a lot better anyways."

"Too hot to go back over there."

"Too hot to get shot too."

"Shu-u-u . . ." he hushed me, peering into the woods beside the trail.

"Deer," I said.

Jubal crouched low and motioned me to move out on the other side as he disappeared behind some huckleberry bushes.

I stooped down and crept through the heavy undergrowth, stopping every few feet to listen. I only heard the sound of insects in the trees, and birds. Lots of birds.

Suddenly, there was an explosion of noise and a scream from the direction Jubal had gone. I ran toward the commotion, branches slapping at my face.

Jubal was under a bush and had a headlock on Squirrel. Squirrel's glasses were on the ground and one shoe was off.

"Let me go!" Squirrel yelled. "I haven't done anything."

"Let him up," I said.

"He was spying on us," said Jubal, tightening his grip.

Squirrel's face was beet red.

"I wasn't spying . . ." he gasped. "I was just . . . just . . ."

"Let him up," I repeated.

Slowly Jubal released his hold, and Squirrel crawled to his feet and brushed the dirt and leaves off his arms. His skin was very pale. There was no way he had more than a gnat's navelful of colored blood if he had any at all, which I strongly doubted.

"I was thinking maybe I might join," Squirrel said, breathing hard. He picked up his glasses, pushed them onto his face, and flicked off a leaf sticking to one of the lenses.

"You had your chance," said Jubal, looking down at Squirrel with a scowl.

"Y'all took me by surprise. I like to have time to consider important, possibly life-altering decisions."

"You're right to do so," I said quickly. "Smart people do that. And we only want smart people in the Scorpions, right, Jubal?"

Jubal didn't reply.

"How much lumber do you need?" asked Squirrel.

"For the walls and roof," I said.

"Don't forget the tin," said Jubal. "To cover the roof. 'Course, it don't have to be new tin. And paint."

"Paint?" I asked. We'd never talked about paint.

"Green and brown," said Jubal. "We gonna paint it camouflage."

"Camouflage?" asked Squirrel.

"To make it hard for our enemies to find us," said Jubal.

"What enemies?"

"Reno McCarthy, for one," I said.

I knew Squirrel couldn't stand Reno any more than me and Jubal could. Reno picked on him at school even worse than he did me. He would slip up behind him in the hallways and goose him. It was so bad Squirrel would sneak away whenever he saw Reno nearby.

"I'll discuss it with my father," said Squirrel. "Where're you going to build this hideout?"

We led him to the site.

He walked around, appraising it, looked to the sky a couple of times, paced off the area in each direction, then said, "Worthy location."

Jubal couldn't help but smile. "I picked it out," he said.

"Where're the plans?" asked Squirrel.

"That's secret," said Jubal, the smile vanishing.

"We ain't drawed up nothing yet," I confessed.

"We don't need no plan," said Jubal. "I got it all right here." He tapped the side of his head.

"Am I supposed to see inside your head?" asked Squirrel. "I can't figure out how much lumber it's going to take without a plan." He looked at the sky again. "It ought to face east. I'll draw up something."

Jubal and I agreed that he could draw out a plan. I rode up to Uncle Chicago's house, borrowed a small sketch pad, a ruler, and a pencil, and returned.

Squirrel sat down on the ground cross-legged and drafted an eight-by-eight-foot cabin with a ceiling six foot high in the front and seven foot high in the back.

"I'll take this home and calculate exactly how many feet of lumber we need," he said.

"What do you think your father will say?" I asked.

He shrugged a shoulder. "I'll explain how much we require and he can subtract that from what he has and compare it to what he figures he'll need."

"I don't suppose we could just go ahead and borrow some," said Jubal. "We wouldn't need all that much."

"No," Squirrel said firmly.

"What's he going to build?" I asked.

"New kennels. I'll let you know what he says in the morning." He started to leave, then paused and grinned at us. "'One for all, and all for one.' I like that."

After he was gone, Jubal said to me, "His father ain't gonna give us no lumber. Nobody ever gives you something for nothing."

"Let's wait and see," I said. "He may surprise you."

FOUR

THAT NIGHT MAMA and my younger sister, Missy, and I went with Poppa to City Park. Twice a week Poppa played softball for the plant. He played outfield, but usually didn't start. He had a bum knee, he said, and it slowed him down a bit. But he could hit the ball a country mile, and the coach put him in to pinch-hit a lot. Poppa's team was scheduled to play the second game, and the first game, between Western Auto and Big Star, was only in the third inning when we arrived.

I walked past the concession trailer, which sold hot dogs, hamburgers, and soft drinks, toward the rest rooms.

The rest rooms were on the back side of the swimming pool at the edge of a creek bank. When I was coming out of the men's, Reno McCarthy and another boy were walking up the sidewalk toward me. I started to move past them.

"Well, well, well," said Reno, stepping in front of me. His lips twisted into a sick-looking smile. "Was

that the white rest room I just seen you coming out of?
I thought maybe you used the colored rest room."

I tried to step around him, but he jabbed me in the
shoulder with his hand and pushed me back.

"I ain't through with you," he said. Then to the
other boy, he said, "This turd tapper likes coloreds
better than white people, Milton. What do you think
about that?"

Milton didn't say anything. He didn't look especially interested in me, either.

"You think coloreds are better than whites?" Reno
said, stepping close to my face and shoving me back
toward the creek bank.

"I ain't looking for trouble," I said, making another
attempt to go around him. I didn't know if I could
outrun him or not. Maybe if I could just sprint beyond
the swimming pool to where there were people I would
be okay. He wouldn't do this around a lot of other
folks.

"You're looking at a real smart boy, Milton," Reno
said, jabbing my shoulder again. "He likes to read all
them stupid books, don't you, turd tapper? But you
ain't that smart. Can you change the points in a car?
Do you even know what points do?"

The reading reference concerned an incident in
class last year. The teacher had called on Reno to read,
and he was stumbling on the simplest words. Everybody started giggling, and I laughed too loud. Then I
looked at Reno. He was glaring at me, and I stopped.

I wished very much I hadn't laughed and probably wouldn't have except everybody else was.

"I ain't that smart," I said. I felt like I had to pee again.

"Milton, I hear he's got this artist uncle who's real strange," Reno said. "And his uncle seems to like coloreds better than whites, too."

"Let's go," Milton said. "I got to take a leak."

"Just a minute. This won't take long." He reached up and took my chin in his hand and squeezed. "I'm telling you this, turd tapper. Your uncle is going to find out what happens to people who turn against their own. And another thing—Jubal Harris is mine. I own him and he is gonna suffer. I can't tell you how bad he's going to hurt, but—"

"We got a problem here?" Poppa's voice came from behind Reno.

Reno dropped his hand from my face and turned around. "Oh . . . Mr. Grant," he said. "We was just horsing around."

Milton backed away.

Poppa stepped right square in front of Reno. "You all right?" he said to me with his eyes still on Reno.

"Yes, sir," I said.

"Seems to me you need to be matched up with somebody your own size," Poppa said, moving his face only inches from Reno's.

"I didn't mean nothing," Reno said. "It was just a joke."

"I'm about your size," Poppa said, moving even closer to Reno. Of course, Poppa was quite a bit bigger.

Reno backed up. "Honest, Mr. Grant. We was playing."

Poppa's eyes narrowed at Reno and he gave a little smile. "Well now, I am glad to hear that, because if I thought otherwise there ain't no telling what I'd do. Are you hearing me?"

"Yes, sir," Reno said.

"Let's go, Cooper," Poppa said, turning back up the sidewalk.

I walked beside him and he put his arm around my shoulders. "Missy was coming to the bathroom and saw those boys with you," he said. "She came to get me."

I didn't say anything.

After we passed the swimming pool, he said, "I could use a hot dog. What about you?"

FIVE

THE NEXT MORNING after I finished my paper route, I told Jubal about my encounter with Reno.

"He's cruising for a bruising," he said.

"He don't think much of you, either."

"I ain't studying him." He spit right after he said this.

We went to Squirrel's house right after breakfast. He told us his father said no on the lumber, that he needed every bit of what he had and maybe more, that besides the new kennels he wasn't sure what all he might need to build.

"Then we got to go to the Montgomery place like I been saying," said Jubal.

I explained to Squirrel about the abandoned houses.

"Did y'all know Mr. Montgomery shot a man dead once?" Squirrel asked.

"It was a knife," I said. "And it was a long time ago."

"Let's go," said Jubal.

Both of them climbed on the scooter behind me and we rode to the hideout site. Jubal led the way as we walked down the hillside toward the old fence.

"I think we should talk more about this," Squirrel said, walking behind me. "Maybe we should vote on it."

Jubal said without looking back, "We ain't letting no chickens into the Scorpions."

"It's not a matter of valor," said Squirrel. "It's discretion."

Jubal walked faster, as if he didn't hear him.

We crossed the fence and fought our way through a maze of vines and brambles. The leaves of the trees overhead completely blocked out the sun and, in the humid shade, mosquitoes hummed around our ears.

In a few minutes, we emerged from the woods onto a field of waist-high shag grass, and I knew I was going to have to spend an hour pulling beggar's-lice off my socks and pants before Mama would let me in the house.

To the left of us was a row of dilapidated share-cropper cabins. Some were missing large sections of their tin roofs. On others the tin was twisted and bent from high winds. The entire front porch of one cabin had collapsed.

"It's the second one," said Jubal.

"What's the second one?" Squirrel asked.

Jubal walked on toward the cabins. "The one my daddy grew up in," he said.

"Where's Mr. Montgomery's house?" I asked, looking around. I thought Squirrel's idea about discretion had a lot to commend it.

"Over that hill," said Jubal. "He can't see us from there."

"Perhaps he would be open to some sort of negotiation," said Squirrel. "Maybe he has some work to be done around here and we could do it in exchange for the materials we need."

"We can get all the tin we need, too," said Jubal.

"Maybe Squirrel's got a point to consider," I said. My mouth was very dry.

Jubal stopped and turned to face both of us. He put his hands on his hips. "Are we Scorpions or what?" he asked.

Squirrel's eyebrows rose. "Does that mean I'm already in?" he asked.

Jubal gave him a hard look, then turned and continued on toward the cabins. We stopped in front of the cabin Marcellus Harris had lived in growing up. Marcellus's mother, Rachel, had been the Montgomerys' cook. The cabin looked in much better condition than the other cabins. None of the tin was missing. In fact, one section looked almost new.

"Have you ever been inside?" I asked.

Jubal shook his head and climbed the front steps. We followed. The old boards groaned beneath our weight.

Jubal led through the front door. The front room

was as wide as the house and had two doorways in the rear wall. The doorway on the right opened to the kitchen. I could see an old wood stove against the back wall. The other door was closed.

Jubal looked around the room. "This is where my father lived," he said softly.

It occurred to me that until yesterday, I hadn't heard Jubal refer to Marcellus since he died.

"Okay, we've seen it," said Squirrel. "Let's go."

Jubal stepped over to the closed door, put his hand on the dark metal doorknob, and turned. The door slowly fell open.

It was a small, narrow room. The ceiling was hardly six foot high. Against the wall was an iron bed on which was a bare mattress. And lying on the mattress was the body of an old man.

SIX

HE WAS WEARING faded overalls without a shirt, and his mouth sagged open.

"Is he dead?" whispered Squirrel.

There was a groan from the man and all three of us jumped.

He raised up and looked at us. His shaggy hair was white and his eyebrows sprayed out in long tangles over his eyes. It was Mr. Montgomery. "What the—" he said, suddenly swinging his feet to the floor and standing up. The hair on his chest and shoulders was as white as the hair on his head. His eyes darted from one to the other of us. "What y'all doing here?"

"Nothing, sir," said Jubal.

The man's eyes were hard and cold and his hands clenched into fists. "I'll teach you nothing, boy," he said through his teeth as he stepped toward Jubal.

Jubal backed away. "I'm Marcellus Harris's son," he said quickly. "Rachel is my grandmother. I'm Jubal."

Mr. Montgomery stopped and cocked his head, looking closely at Jubal. "What do you want?" he asked.

"Nothing, sir."

The man held his eyes on Jubal for a long moment, then blinked and looked at me. "And who are you?" he asked.

"Cooper Grant, sir," I said.

He stretched his back slightly and put his hands on his hips. "You're Angus's boy?"

"Yes, sir."

"And who's that trying to sneak out the door over there?"

"It's me," said Squirrel, "but I'm not trying to sneak out."

"Don't lie to me, boy. I can't abide liars."

"I'm Aaron Kogan, sir. I live across the road."

Mr. Montgomery made some sort of a grunt, then looked at Jubal again. "I shoot people who trespass on my land. Now, tell me what y'all doing here. And I can tell if you lying."

"Exploring," said Jubal. "We didn't mean no harm."

"You didn't come to steal my chickens? Now don't lie to me, boy."

"No, sir," said Jubal. "We ain't seen no chickens."

"I'll shoot anybody messes with my chickens, too."

Squirrel cleared his throat. "You wouldn't have any old lumber you didn't want, would you?"

"Old lumber?"

"I just wanted to look around in here," Jubal said quietly.

"Look around for what?"

"Nothing."

Mr. Montgomery continued to stare at Jubal. He nodded his head slowly and gave another little grunt. "You favor your daddy some."

"So folks say."

"What kind of lumber you wanting?"

"We're building a cabin," I said. "Just some old boards—"

"I didn't ask you," Mr. Montgomery interrupted. "I was asking him."

"We're making a cabin back in the woods," Jubal said. "Maybe some of them boards off these old falling down houses. We need some tin, too."

"What are you making a cabin for?"

"We just wants a cabin for a clubhouse."

Mr. Montgomery's eyes were fixed on Jubal. He seemed to have relaxed more. He said, "How old you now?"

"Thirteen."

"Cabin, eh?" He glanced at me, then Squirrel, then gave a snort. "Well now, if you three don't make a sight."

"We don't need much," said Jubal.

Mr. Montgomery scratched his chin. "I'll have to study on it. How much y'all willing to pay?"

"We ain't got no money," said Jubal.

"I didn't think you did."

"We could do some work for you," said Squirrel.

"I'm talking with him, not you," Mr. Montgomery said to Squirrel.

"You got anything you need us to do for you?" asked Jubal.

"Maybe," he said slowly. "Maybe I do. But, like I said, I need to study on it. I want y'all to come back tomorrow. Nine o'clock."

"We can work hard," said Squirrel.

Mr. Montgomery ignored him and looked at Jubal. "How's Rachel?" he asked.

"She's fine."

"I still miss her biscuits."

"She don't cook much no more."

"Yes, of course," said Mr. Montgomery.

He moved past Jubal slowly, a bit unsteadily, as he walked out the front door and onto the porch. Jubal followed and stood beside him. Squirrel and I, walking as softly as we could, joined them.

Mr. Montgomery stepped down onto the top step, then reached his fingers into the top pocket of his overalls and withdrew a pocketknife. It was well worn and had a bone handle. He held it out to Jubal.

"Go on. Take it," he said.

"Sir?" asked Jubal.

"I said take it."

Jubal took the knife.

Mr. Montgomery descended one step at a time, and started up the path, then paused and looked back at us. "Tomorrow morning at nine o'clock," he said. "And don't say nothing about being here and talking with me. No telling what that crazy son of mine would do to you. Ike don't like people coming on our land."

"Yes, sir," we all said at the same time.

After he was gone, I said to Jubal, "How come he give you that knife?"

"'Cause he felt like it, I suppose."

"And you said don't nobody ever give you anything."

"I said ain't nobody going to give you something for nothing."

"What's that suppose to mean?"

"It means what it means," he said, opening the pocketknife. The blade was sharp and long.

"You think that's what he killed that man with?" I asked.

"Probably."

"What do you reckon he'll have us do?" Squirrel asked.

"He's probably gonna make us weed his garden or something," said Jubal, slipping the knife into his pocket.

"He didn't look like a killer to me," Squirrel said.

Jubal chuckled. "And just how many killers you seen?"

"I only meant—"

"Let's go," said Jubal, walking back toward the field of shag grass.

SEVEN

BOTH JUBAL AND SQUIRREL had to work that afternoon. Jubal worked for Mrs. Pouncey, a woman who lived in a big two-story house in town. He took care of her yard, and had been working for her for two years. Another woman at the beginning of the summer had offered him more money to work for her, but Jubal turned her down. He told me he wanted to stay with Mrs. Pouncey because she was a widow woman, and she didn't have anybody else to help her at all.

Squirrel worked at his father's five-and-ten-cent store two afternoons a week. Squirrel said his father expected him to run the store someday after he retired, but Squirrel was planning to join the FBI. That would be, of course, after he finished playing for the St. Louis Cardinals. Squirrel loved baseball, but he wasn't no better than me. He wasn't going to play for the Cardinals any more than I was. In fact, I wasn't interested because I figured I'd be playing for the Pittsburgh Steelers maybe.

After finishing my paper route that morning, I was free to do whatever I wanted for the rest of the day. That afternoon, I went swimming at the city pool for an hour. There were only a few younger kids there, nobody my age. Then I watched TV till Jubal got off work and returned to the house so we could work out.

I had set three goals for myself that summer. One was to get our Scorpions clubhouse built. The second was to paint a picture that would win first place in the fifteen-and-under art competition at the county fair in October. And the third was to get big and strong enough to beat out Reno for the first team center on the football team.

We both played for Colbert Junior High and, since Reno had been held back two grades already, were both going into the eighth grade. Last season Reno was second team and played a little.

I was third team and only got in one game. That was at Pontotoc when our team was ahead by thirty-three points. Coach Turner turned to the bench and yelled, "Who ain't been in yet?"

I raised my hand, and he jerked his thumb toward the field. I grabbed my helmet.

"Hit somebody, Tiger!" he hollered after me.

Coach called everybody on the third team Tiger. He called the boys on the first and second teams by their names. Always the last name. I don't think he knew the names of any of us on the third team. Come fall, I wanted to hear him yell out to me, "Grant, get in there and knock somebody's head off!"

Jubal was also going into the eighth grade, only at Washington. It was the only school for coloreds in town, and it ran from first grade through high school. They didn't have a junior high team, but Jubal was big enough to have already played in six games for their high school team last season. Besides, most of the older colored boys had already dropped out of school to work full time, so a lot of eighth and ninth graders got to play.

We worked out with a set of weights Poppa made for us out of iron water pipes and various sized concrete-filled tin cans. The heaviest weight was sixty pounds, and Jubal could do three sets of ten reps without even breaking a sweat.

I was sitting on the front steps waiting for him when he walked up the path, whittling on a stick. "You know," he said right off. "What we should have done was just ask him to let us have that cabin for our hideout."

"What? You crazy? Why would he give us a cabin? We're lucky he's going to let us work some lumber off him."

Jubal folded his knife and slipped it into his pocket and smiled. "Why don't we go back over there after supper and select our boards?" he said. "We only want to get the best."

"Let's work out," I said, standing up. "The man

said to meet him at nine in the morning, and that's what we are going to do."

Jubal shrugged one shoulder. "Never hurts to ask," he said.

We worked with the weights till Glory called us to supper. Mama let Jubal and his sister, Alvina, eat in the kitchen each night with Glory while we ate in the dining room. Sometimes, like tonight, I ate with Jubal in the kitchen.

Alvina, I should mention, was small and wiry and never moved like a normal person, but was more like a wasp, flitting here and there, zipping around. I called her "Fly."

At the table, Jubal took out his knife and laid it beside his plate.

Alvina's eyes jumped on that knife at once. "Where'd you get that?" she demanded.

Glory was just coming in from the dining room. "Get what?" she asked.

Jubal quickly pulled the knife off the table and held it in his lap.

"Let me see that," Glory said.

Jubal put it into his pocket. "It's mine," he said.

"You stole it, didn't you?" said Alvina.

Glory hurried to the oven and took out a pan of corn bread. "I ain't through with you," she said to Jubal as she went back into the dining room.

He grinned at Alvina but said nothing.

"You stole it," she repeated.

"Did I steal it?" he asked me.

"No," I said, wishing he'd not gotten me into this. Next thing, Poppa was going to find out I'd been over on the Montgomerys' land and all Hades was going to break out.

Glory came back and stood in front of Jubal with her hands on her hips. Her lower lip pouted out as it always did when she was very cross. "Now, you put back on the table whatever it was you had there," she said.

Jubal slowly took out the knife and placed it gently on the tabletop beside his plate.

"So?" she demanded.

"A man gave it to me."

"Now, don't you lie to me, boy. This is your mother. What man?"

"Mr. Gideon Montgomery."

Glory's eyes widened out. "Where'd you see Mr. Gideon?"

"We went over to see the house Daddy growed up in."

She looked at me for confirmation.

I nodded my head. "That's right. He just gave him the knife. Jubal didn't ask for it or nothing."

Glory looked at Jubal for a long time, then said, "All right. If Mr. Gideon give it to you, I ain't got nothing else to say about it. But y'all stay away from that place. You hear me?"

She moved back to the stove and began heaping turnip greens from the pot into a serving bowl.

Jubal smirked at his sister.

"Cut that out," said Glory, without turning around. "I mean it. And that man don't owe you nothing. Stay away from him. Now, Alvina, you say the blessing."

EIGHT

FRIDAY MORNING Jubal, Squirrel, and I walked back across the field on Mr. Montgomery's land to the row of cabins. We were plenty early because we didn't want to make him upset.

"I sure don't want to pull weeds out in this sun, if that's what he's got in mind," said Jubal.

"We'll do whatever we have to do to get that lumber and tin," I said, very grateful that we didn't need to risk getting shot by taking it without permission.

"I think this approach is best," said Squirrel. "Everything needs to be on the up and up."

We arrived at the cabin where Rachel and Marcellus lived all those long years ago. Mr. Montgomery was sitting on the porch in a straight-backed chair.

"I was about to give up on you boys," he said, with a slight smile.

"It's not quite nine yet," said Squirrel, looking at his watch.

"My, my, if you ain't smart enough to tell time," said Mr. Montgomery.

"I only meant—"

"You ain't ever on time for me, boy," said Mr. Montgomery. He looked at Jubal. "You ain't lost my knife, has you?"

"No, sir. I ain't lost *my* knife."

Mr. Montgomery smiled and motioned us to come up onto the porch.

"Now," he said, once we were all in front of him. "I've been giving this matter a lot of consideration." He lifted his hand and pointed at the cabins to the right. "You see that one with the porch caved in? That's the one you can have the lumber off of."

"And tin," said Jubal.

"And tin," he said. He looked at us for a few moments, smiling. Then, he said, "And this is what I want from you." He now turned his eyes on Jubal. "I can't drive anymore, you see. And I'm mighty hungry for some of Rachel's biscuits. I want you boys to take me to her place tomorrow morning."

"Sir?" asked Jubal. He was as taken aback as I was.

Mr. Montgomery smiled. "I just want to see her and eat some of those hot biscuits and redeye gravy of hers one more time 'fore I die."

"I got to work for Mrs. Pouncey in the morning," Jubal said.

"And I got art class," I said.

"I got to work till noon," said Squirrel.

"Then what time can y'all be here?" asked Mr. Montgomery.

Jubal and I looked at each other. "Eleven?" I suggested.

Jubal nodded.

"Like I said, I have to work till noon," said Squirrel.

"Then eleven it is," said Mr. Montgomery, putting his hands on his knees and pushing himself up. "And y'all can take all the tin and boards you want. I think there's a table in that place too. You can have it. Whatever you want. *After* I see Rachel."

He held tightly onto one of the porch posts and descended the steps one at a time. He paused when he reached the ground, swayed slightly, then started up the path toward his own house.

Jubal walked fast across the field, and we hurried to keep pace with him. "This is nuts," he said. "Grandma don't cook no more. She don't even know what year this is."

"It's just biscuits," I said.

"She don't even have flour," said Jubal. "How she gonna make biscuits?"

"Maybe we should go talk to her, kind of get her thinking about it," I said.

"Perhaps we could just buy some biscuits at Tony's Cafe and take them to him," suggested Squirrel.

"I don't think that would be exactly on the up and up, do you?" said Jubal. "Besides, he knows her biscuits."

Squirrel didn't reply.

We entered the woods, crossed the fence at the site for the Scorpions' Lair, and reached my scooter on the road.

"Maybe we could sneak some flour and stuff and take it to her," I said. "There's plenty in the kitchen."

"I got to think about it," Jubal said, getting on back right behind me.

"Why do I always have to sit on the very back," said Squirrel. "I keep almost falling off."

"Get on or walk," said Jubal.

We rode to the quarters, parked at Jubal's house, and walked to his grandmother's cabin. Her cabin was in the woods a short ways from the quarters.

She was sitting on the front porch in her rocker, fanning herself with a paper fan that had a picture of Jesus on it. We stood on the ground in front of her.

She was rail thin, dark skinned, and had red-streaked eyes. She rarely left her cabin, and the thick woods pressed in on all sides. Glory cooked her food and washed her clothes.

"Where's my dinner?" she said, frowning at Jubal.

"It ain't time yet, Grandma. We was wondering if you ever does any cooking anymore."

"I'm a good cook," she said. Then she looked at me. "And Miss Sarah ain't got no right to let me go. I'm a good cook. You tell her that."

"This ain't Ike, Grandma. It's Cooper."

"And who is that?" she asked. She was chewing a black gum snuff stick.

"That's Squirrel," said Jubal. "And he ain't as white as he looks."

She looked at me again, then said, "Mr. Gideon swears by my cooking."

"What about biscuits and gravy?" asked Jubal. "Can you make some of that?"

"Of course," she snapped at him. "That's one of my specialties. Now, Mr. Gideon like his biscuits and gravy most of all with scrambled eggs and squirrel brains." She paused and looked at me again. "Y'all need to bring me some squirrels. I can't make no scrambled eggs and squirrel brains without squirrels."

"Do you think you could make some biscuits for Mr. Gideon?" asked Jubal. "I mean, if he was to come here. I mean like if he was to come here tomorrow?"

She smiled and her eyes sparkled. "Don't you worry none about what I can cook or not cook." Then she frowned. "You boys leave them melons alone, you hear?"

As we walked back, Squirrel said, "What melons? What's she talking about?"

"She'll probably burn the house down if she tries to build a fire in that stove," Jubal said.

"What melons?" Squirrel repeated.

"What all is she gonna need for the biscuits?" I asked.

Jubal didn't reply.

NINE

SATURDAY MORNING I finished my route by 6:30. Jubal was waiting for me in front of our barn. Each morning, except Sundays, we ran three miles together over a course we'd marked out across the bottom and along an old logging road not far from Uncle Chicago's place until it climbed Rattlesnake Hill. The air was cool with day just breaking as we began running.

"I got all the stuff," Jubal said. "I'll take it over to Grandma this morning. Then I'll be by Mr. James's to get you right when y'all done." Mr. James was Uncle Chicago, my mother's brother. Everybody called him Chicago except colored folks and my grandmother Nana.

After we ran, Jubal went home, and I went to Uncle Chicago's for art. Every Saturday morning, he taught art to me and Alvina.

He lived at the end of a graveled road on the west side of our land, not far from the site for the

Scorpions' Lair. It was a house he'd built himself, wood frame, and was mostly a studio, cluttered with easels, shelves of art supplies, and paintings in various stages of completion.

"Just putting the eggs on," he called from the kitchen as I walked in. "Sit down and drink your orange juice."

I laid the newspaper at his place and sat down on the opposite side of the table. I brought Uncle Chicago his paper every morning after I finished my route, and during the summertime, I stayed for breakfast.

"A lot more COFO people coming," he said, reading the paper. "About 280 more."

The Council of Federated Organizations was made up of several groups, including the National Association for the Advancement of Colored People, the Student Nonviolent Coordinating Committee, and the Congress of Racial Equality. The people who were coming were mostly college students from the north who were going to spend the summer in Mississippi helping the coloreds get registered to vote. The *Daily Journal* referred to them as civil rights workers, and Uncle Chicago talked about it a lot.

All the white people I knew, except Uncle Chicago, of course, were terribly upset about it, and said they ought to stay put. Uncle Chicago was convinced that some of these COFO volunteers were going to get killed. But whether they came or not made little difference to me. What I wanted to know about was Gideon Montgomery.

"Tell me about Gideon Montgomery," I said, not knowing any other way to get to the subject.

"What about him?"

I thought about telling him about going to see the cabin where Marcellus grew up and that Mr. Montgomery was going to give us all the lumber and tin we needed just for taking him to Auntie Rachel's to eat biscuits, but decided maybe I shouldn't. He might slip up and tell Mama and then there'd be the devil to pay.

Instead, I said, "We're building our clubhouse right near his land, and I was just wondering."

"Stay off his place. They're rough people. His wife was the sister of Toby McCarthy's father. You know what kind of a man Toby is." I knew. He was Reno's father.

"That means Mr. Montgomery's son, Ike, and Toby are cousins?" I asked.

"Yes, but there's no love lost between them," he said. "Just stay away from there."

The front screen door scraped open.

"Ah," said Uncle Chicago with a smile. "The queen is here. We can begin."

Alvina smiled back at him. She didn't greet me, but then she rarely did.

Uncle Chicago had called her the Queen of Sheba, or simply "the queen," for as long as I could remember.

And, little runt that she was, I noticed she straightened her shoulders and tried to appear taller whenever he called her that.

Uncle Chicago had class with us every Saturday morning for two hours. He'd been teaching me since I was eight and Alvina for the last two years. Uncle Chicago said it would be good for me to have someone pushing me, that working by myself as the only student could make me sluggish, that I needed someone like a fly to sting my butt once in a while to wake me up.

We did drawing exercises first—gesture, contour, and recall drawing. Bessie arrived just as we were beginning to paint in oil.

Bessie was an artist too, and had taught art at the colored school for almost forty years. I wasn't sure how old Bessie was, but I knew she was as old as Nana, who was in her sixties, since they were playmates as children. Bessie didn't act old, though. And for a big woman, she moved very fast. Drove fast, talked fast, walked fast.

She had a broad face and a smile that sometimes seemed wider than her face. Whenever she saw me, she grinned and winked as if to assure me that we shared something together that no one else knew about.

Uncle Chicago reminded me on occasion that Bessie was his first art teacher. When he was small, Bessie used to baby-sit him, and she had him drawing before he was three. When he was a student at the art institute, she sent him a little money every week to help out.

Bessie was wearing a flowing pale yellow dress, dangling earrings, and a bright yellow scarf around her head. You never saw Bessie without something bright on.

"Sit. Sit," Uncle Chicago said to her, escorting her onto the model's platform and into the chair.

"I met a white minister from New Jersey in Meridian the other day," she said. "Can you imagine? He's seventy-three and coming down here to work with COFO for the summer."

"I thought it was just college students," I said.

"Thinking requires something more than mush brains," Alvina said to me under her breath.

"Shut up, Fly," I said.

"Let's try this," Uncle Chicago said, holding out a wide-brimmed straw hat to Bessie.

She laughed and said, "No, thank you. You want me to look like a washerwoman?"

Bessie definitely didn't want to look like a washerwoman. She was college educated, and, when she wanted to, she could talk just like a white person. On the phone, she told me, she sometimes talked like that when trying to get repairmen to come to her house.

Uncle Chicago stepped back and put his hands

together, studying her. "Okay," he said. "I like the scarf better anyway. Let's paint, now."

We set up our palettes and began blocking her in.

Bessie shifted in her seat.

"Be still," said Uncle Chicago. "Give these kids a decent chance of catching your likeness."

She laughed. "They'd better be flattering me. Alvina, don't make me a day over fifty. Same for you, Cooper. How long do I have to sit?"

"Not long," Uncle Chicago said, placing a stretched canvas on his easel.

We painted about an hour. Then Bessie said she was tired of sitting, and got up.

"I got something else I want to paint," said Alvina. She put down her brush and walked across the room to the bag in the chair. She took out a framed photograph and held it up for us to see.

It was her father, Marcellus.

Uncle Chicago smiled a closed-mouth smile. There was sadness in his eyes.

"I think that will make a nice painting," he said.

Bessie looked at the picture, then walked to the door.

"Wait," said Uncle Chicago.

She shook her head. I could see she was upset. And, without saying anything else, she left the house.

"Finish up from memory," he said to us.

We worked in silence for a while longer.

Jubal arrived at the end of class, just as we were

cleaning up. "Hurry up," he said to me as I wiped down my palette with turpentine.

After Uncle Chicago inspected my palette and brushes, he dismissed me. Alvina wasn't quite through. The clock on the kitchen wall said 10:41.

Jubal broke into a half trot as soon as we got outside.

"We got plenty of time," I said, running after him.

"I want to be there 'fore him this time," he said.

We reached the house in ten minutes. Mr. Montgomery was not sitting on the front porch.

Jubal stood at the door and called out, "Mr. Gideon?"

No answer.

Jubal smiled at me. "We beat him," he said.

We sat down on the steps and waited for a while. Then, the rumble of a vehicle grew closer. We both stood up. A pickup topped the rise on the trail coming down toward the cabins.

"I thought he couldn't drive," Jubal said.

"That's Ike's truck," I said.

We darted into the cabin.

"I think he saw us," I said, breathing fast and looking around the front room.

"The back door," said Jubal.

Then we both froze.

Mr. Montgomery was lying on the bed like he'd been the first time we came. He was wearing a starched white shirt, dark slacks, and a maroon necktie. One arm dangled from the bed. In his other hand he held a bouquet of pink roses.

The front door banged open and Ike stepped into the room. "What are you boys doing in here?" he said.

"He . . . he told us to meet him," I said, pointing toward the bedroom.

Ike brushed past us and stepped to the side of the bed. "Daddy?" he said, shaking the old man's shoulder. "Da—"

He picked up Mr. Montgomery's arm and felt his wrist.

Then he looked up at us. I can't describe the look in his eyes.

Jubal said, "We just found him like tha-"

"Get out!" said Ike. "Get out, and I don't want to ever see you on this property again. Get going!"

We left quickly.

"Mr. Gideon good as gave us that lumber," said Jubal as we walked back across the field. "We went to all that trouble to take Grandma the stuff for the biscuits and came to get him. It ain't our fault he up and died and didn't keep his part of the bargain. That tin and lumber is rightfully ours."

"I really don't think this is a good time to take it," I said.

"I didn't mean right now. But I do mean to get it. It's ours."

TEN

JUBAL SAID that he had to return to Mrs. Pouncey's after lunch.

"But this is Saturday," I said. Jubal didn't have to work on Saturday afternoons.

"She's got her preacher coming for dinner after church tomorrow and she ain't near 'bout finished cleaning up her house. She said she could get it all done herself but I know she can't. She gets tired out real easy."

I went on home. I didn't say anything to the folks about us finding Mr. Montgomery. I needed to think how I was going to explain us going there. We hadn't really done anything wrong, but I knew Poppa wouldn't like the idea of me going onto the Montgomery place, period. And, I expected Ike Montgomery was going to arrive at any minute and tell him.

I wanted to get away from the house, so I dug up a canful of red worms in the moist dirt by the side of the barn and went down to the pond. I sat in the shade of some pines just east of the dam and fished.

I noticed Poppa walk out to the barn several times over the next two hours. He didn't check on the dogs once. Then he got into his pickup and drove off.

Maybe Ike phoned.

I caught a large strawberry bream. And then another and another. Every time I threw my line out, I got a strike.

An hour later I was in the kitchen cleaning the mess of bream when I heard Poppa's truck pull up beside the house. He jerked open the back door and stepped into the kitchen. "Where the devil have you been?" he said to me. His speech was slightly slurred.

"Fishing," I said, as I ran the filleting knife down the side of a large bream.

"There was a meeting," he said. "At Wrightson's."

"A meeting?" I asked. I didn't have any idea what he was talking about. A lot of times when he'd been drinking he didn't make a lot of sense.

"And Bill Turner was asking about you. He wanted to know how come you weren't there."

"Coach Turner?" I asked. "He asked about me?"

"There were a couple of other boys on your team there. Bill introduced them. He asked me if you were coming out for football this year."

"I'm going out," I said. "Doesn't he know that? Why would he ask that?"

"I guess because you weren't there."

"Who were the boys?" I asked.

"Moses Jackson's boy and George Simmons's boy."

"I didn't know about it," I said. "What kind of meeting?"

Mama came into the room. "I didn't hear you come in," she said to Poppa.

"Gideon Montgomery died," he told her. "Died in his sleep, Ike said."

"You saw Ike?" I asked.

"No. But he phoned before I left to tell me. He said he couldn't make the meeting."

"Is that all he said? I mean . . ."

Poppa looked at me curiously. Then he said to Mama, "They're going to funeralize him Monday."

"I'll take him a dish this evening," Mama said.

Poppa grunted something I didn't understand and swayed out of the room and down the hallway.

ELEVEN

SUNDAY MORNING, I waited on the front porch for Bessie. She was running late, as usual. I don't think in all my life she'd ever picked me up on time.

Mama and Poppa didn't go to church, except a couple of times a year when Missy's choir was singing. Poppa always wore his tie, which he hated almost as much as he hated being around all those hypocrite rich people, he told me. But he went anyways because Missy asked him to. All the other parents would be there, she said. Nana was Pentecostal, but she didn't go anymore at all.

Mama said when Missy and I were real little, Bessie asked if she could take us to Sunday school at her church, since we didn't go anywhere, and I'd been going to church with her ever since.

Missy started going to First Baptist with a friend three years ago, but I liked my church and didn't plan to go anyplace else.

Bessie's '52 Ford jerked to a stop in front of the

house. Dust rose all around the car. It had been extra dry and hot for several days. Mama said her garden was withering up and for me to pray at church for rain.

Bessie was dressed all in pink—pink dress and floppy pink hat—and wore a pair of dangling gold earrings I hadn't seen before. "Let's go, let's go," she said as I got in the car.

As we sped past the Montgomery mailbox, I glanced up the narrow dirt lane leading toward the house. The house itself couldn't be seen from the road because of the trees.

"Mr. Montgomery died," I said.

"He was the very worst sort," she said. "And here he gets the nice luxury of dying in his old age in bed."

"What do you mean?"

"No matter," she said, speeding up.

We had to go the long way to church, through the Taylor community and doubling back on Shubuta Road, because the short way on Oak Grove Road across Bear Creek bottom had a bridge that washed out last winter. The short way was only two and a half miles while the long way was fifteen miles or better.

She turned up the one-lane road that dead-ended at the church. Banks of dust-covered kudzu blurred past. She didn't slow up one bit as we bounced across the plank bridge over the little stream only fifty yards from the church house. She braked to a jerking stop beside a pickup truck.

Bessie taught Sunday school for the youth, which

was sixth grade through high school. Jubal and I always sat together with the boys on one side of the room and the girls sat on the other. The room was especially hot that morning, and Alvina seemed more intent than usual on showing out by answering every question Bessie asked.

Reverend Graham stuck his head in the door just as we were getting started and smiled at us, then said to Bessie, "You need to see me?"

She told us she'd just be a minute and then went out into the hallway to speak with the reverend. I could see them talking, or rather, Bessie talking to him, her mouth close to his ear, and he was frowning.

Jubal leaned his head close to mine. "I think we need to get that lumber today," he said.

"What about bottle collecting?"

"After," he said, giving me a light tap on the knee. "For all I know that crazy Ike will burn down them cabins just to get rid of them."

Bessie stepped back into the room. "Now," she said. "Who can say the memory verse?"

In the worship service, Jubal and I sat in one of the back pews. Bessie sat near the front with several women friends of hers. Like Bessie, they all wore large hats. Some were floppy and wide like hers. Some were just tall. Many of them sparkled with sequins.

As he usually did on Sunday morning, Reverend Graham said we should pray for the families of the four girls—Carole, Denise, Addie Mae, and Cynthia—who were killed when their church in Birmingham was bombed last September. We also prayed for the family of Medgar Evers, who was shot dead in his driveway in Jackson last summer.

Reverend Graham preached about Moses leading the children of Israel into the Promised Land. Somehow, no matter where he started with his Bible text, he always managed to get back around to Moses. And the more he talked about Moses the more excited he got.

Men and women all over the church started standing up and calling out to him, encouraging him, blessing him.

And the more excited he got, the more he sweated. Sweat flicked off his head like he was a prizefighter, and he kept mopping his face with a small towel.

Suddenly, he paused and became very still. "And now I wants to tell you about Gabriel," he said. His voice was low and urgent.

People who were standing one by one began to sit down.

"The angel Gabriel is God Almighty's own very special messenger," he said, moving from behind the pulpit and stepping down onto the floor. "When God wanted the Virgin Mary to know about the little baby boy she was going to have, he sent Gabriel to tell her. Yes, he did. That's because God knows that people knows what Gabriel has to say is going to happen. Yes, it is."

The congregation was strangely quiet, nobody giving any of the usual responses at all. Everybody was leaning forward to hear better. Every eye was riveted on the pastor.

Reverend Graham moved slowly up the aisle, looking first at the folks on one side, and then at those on the other. "And now I have a word from Gabriel," he said, stopping beside a pew. He reached across Mrs. Avery, a very large woman in a pale blue dress, and put his hand on her oldest son, Brelove.

Brelove Avery taught history at the colored school. Jubal thought he was too hard, but Alvina adored him. She was always saying things Mr. Avery said about African kings and queens and empires and such.

"The angel Gabriel has brought a warning," Reverend Graham said. "Terror and destruction are coming for someone. Gabriel say somebody better leave and leave quick!" Reverend Graham wheeled about and headed back to the pulpit.

Brelove Avery got up out of his seat and hurried up the aisle and out the front door. Mrs. Avery let out a loud moan.

After church people were handing money to Mrs. Avery. "See that he gets this," said one old white-headed man, pressing two crumpled dollar bills into her hand.

Mrs. Avery was crying, and several women were standing beside her with their hands on her shoulders.

Bessie drove home a little slower than she had driven to church.

"Why did Brelove Avery leave?" I asked her as soon as we turned onto Shubuta Road.

"The angel Gabriel brought a message," she said. Her eyes were bright and she was smiling.

"What message?" I asked.

"Listen to me," she said. "I know you like to go play with Jubal a lot in the evenings. But tonight I want you to stay away from the quarters. Do you understand?"

"Why?"

"Just do what I say now. Do you understand?" She emphasized each of the words in *Do you understand*.

TWELVE

AFTER LUNCH I went to Jubal's. We got together every Sunday afternoon to gather empty whiskey bottles along the roads. It was our cash crop. I had phoned Squirrel to invite him to join us, but nobody answered the phone.

Jubal had just finished eating, and Glory had a plate for him to take to his grandmother.

As we walked along the trail, I asked, "Where's Brelove Avery going?"

"Don't know," said Jubal. "And don't really care. I ain't never liked history much no way."

"You really believe the angel Gabriel came and talked to Reverend Graham?"

"I don't know no more than you," said Jubal. "And don't say nothing to my grandmother about us finding Mr. Gideon like that."

"Ain't you going to tell her?"

"Yes, but I want to do it easy. She don't need no big shocks at her age."

"How old is she?"

"She won't say, but she be way up there."

When we arrived at her cabin, she wasn't sitting on the porch like she normally was, and smoke was coming out of the chimney.

Jubal walked into the house and I followed.

Auntie Rachel was dressed in a yellow Sunday dress and standing in front of the stove cooking and singing. She looked up at us.

"Now don't you boys mess up nothing," she said. "I got the house all cleaned up. Mr. Gideon is coming. Now, y'all just run on."

"Here's your plate, Grandma," said Jubal, placing the covered dish on the table.

He stood there for a moment, looking at her like he was ready to go ahead and tell her Mr. Gideon was dead, but before he could, she looked at us and frowned. "Was that you boys that stole them melons?" she asked.

"No'm," said Jubal.

"Don't lie to me, boy."

"I ain't lying. Mama said to tell you to eat this before it gets cold."

She cocked her head and looked at me. "Ike, is he lying to me?"

"I'm Cooper," I said.

"Cooper?" she said, wrinkling up her nose. Then she smiled. "Of course. You've told me that before, ain't you? I know your folks."

"And Mama wants to know if you got some laundry that needs doing," said Jubal. "And, about Mr. Gideon . . . he might be delayed."

"Real delayed," I mumbled.

"I better not find out y'all be selling Mr. Gideon's melons." She looked at Jubal, then back to me. "I shore don't need Miss Sarah coming down on me 'bout no melons. And how come he might be delayed?"

"He just might be," said Jubal. "So don't start cooking yet."

"I done started."

Jubal went into the bedroom, bundled up her dirty clothes, and came out.

"Let's go," he said. As we walked down the front steps, he called back to her, "And be sure to eat while it's hot."

"Tell your grandmother I asked after her, Cooper," she said.

After we were away from the house, I said, "That was easy all right. You ain't really told her he's dead."

"She don't really understand who's dead and who's alive nohow."

We hurried back along the trail.

"How come she thought I was Ike?" I asked.

"She sometimes think I'm Daddy," he said. "Mama say old people like that. They move in and out of the past."

We started collecting the whiskey bottles on Oak

Grove Road because, since the bridge was out and nobody drove through anymore, a lot of parkers stopped there on Friday and Saturday nights. Jubal walked along the ditch on one side and I walked the other. Each of us had a croker sack to put the bottles in. We got a nickel a bottle from Mr. Thomas Strickland, a bootlegger.

It was so scorching hot that we decided to take a break from collecting and go for a swim in the creek. The creek water was much cooler than the pond and felt real good. Afterward, when we finished dressing and were climbing the bank beside the washed out bridge, I noticed a car parked on the road above us.

The driver's door opened and Reno McCarthy got out. I wondered what he thought about his great uncle, Mr. Montgomery, dying, but I certainly wasn't going to ask him.

He had a .22 lever action rifle in his hand. He looked at Jubal, then at me, and grinned. "Having a little swim, boys?" he asked.

"Yeah," I said, "and there's almost enough water left for you to go soak your head."

Reno made a face as if he were trying to think of a response. Jubal stepped up onto the road and kept his eyes downcast.

We had left our croker sacks with bottles up under a tree on the other side of the road. Jubal walked toward the tree.

I heard the click of the rifle's lever as Reno loaded a round into the chamber. "I didn't hear you answer me, boy," he said.

Jubal stopped but didn't turn around.

I looked back at Reno. "What's your problem?" I said.

"I didn't hear no answer from him. I was asking you both." He held the rifle on his hip.

Jubal still didn't move or speak.

Reno came forward, circling until he was facing Jubal. In spite of the fact that Reno was two years older, he was half a head shorter.

Jubal wasn't looking at the ground now, but straight down into the eyes of Reno.

Reno held the gun with both hands, one finger on the trigger, and placed the muzzle against the side of Jubal's face. His grin became bigger. "So tell me, boy," he said. "Are we about to piss in our pants or what?" He gave a little giggle.

Quick as the strike of a cottonmouth, Jubal's hand flew up from his side and grabbed the barrel of the rifle. He ripped it out of Reno's hands and threw it over his shoulder. It landed a few feet from the car.

Reno gasped and stepped back. "What do you think you're doing?" he said. "That's a brand new gun and you've slung it in the dirt."

Jubal's face was hard and his fists clenched.

Reno circled around slowly, then bent down to the

ground with his eyes still on Jubal, grabbed the gun and got into the car, all in one swift motion.

Jubal and I stepped to the side of the road as Reno backed around. He leaned out the window and said, "You gonna pay. Both of you."

Then he raced away, tires spinning and dust exploding into the air. We shut our eyes tight and turned our backs. I could hear the car whining through the gears as Reno put distance between himself and us.

I drew a big breath and picked up the sacks. "That might not have been the smartest thing you've ever done," I said.

Jubal glared at me. "I'm a Scorpion," he said. "Nobody messes with a Scorpion. Ain't that right?"

"Yes, but—"

"'One for all, and all for one.' Right?"

I nodded. "Right."

"Come over after supper and we'll go get them boards," he said.

That was not something I looked forward to at all.

THIRTEEN

WHEN I GOT HOME Mama was fixing peanut butter and jelly sandwiches for supper like she did most Sunday nights. We always had sandwiches on weekends when Glory was off. No one else was in the kitchen. Again I wondered if Ike had come by to tell about Jubal and me being on his land and him finding us in the cabin with Mr. Montgomery, but Mama didn't say anything or look upset, so I figured maybe Ike was too busy right now getting ready for the funeral. I said, "I went with Jubal to take his grandmother dinner. I think she's a little out of her mind."

"Auntie Rachel is a nice person. She was always kind to us when we were little."

"At first she thought I was Ike Montgomery and that Jubal was Marcellus and that we stole some melons."

Mama smiled. "When they were little, you never saw Ike without Marcellus being with him. And, most times, your uncle was right there alongside them. Those boys could get into more mischief."

We all ate in the front room, watching some movie on television my dumb sister, Missy, and Nana were keen on. They watched television every night till bedtime. We had an antenna but we only got the Tupelo station good. Tupelo was the biggest town in north Mississippi and only twenty-three miles away.

"Going over to Jubal's for a little while," I said after I finished. I was heading toward the kitchen and the back door.

"Don't be long," Mama called after me.

"What?" said Poppa. He was starting out the back door himself, probably toward the barn. He went out to the barn every night after supper for a while. He said he was going to check on the dogs, and he did. He would talk to his hounds in the kennel like they were little children. But then he'd go into the barn. He spent a lot more time in the barn than he did with the dogs. He didn't know I knew where 'bouts in the tool shed he kept his bottle.

"Where are you going?" he asked me.

"Jubal's."

He let the screen close and stepped toward me. "Not tonight," he said. "You ain't going anywheres tonight."

Mama looked at him questioningly but didn't say anything. She didn't like to cross Poppa, especially on

Sunday after he'd made several trips out to check on the dogs.

"I just don't want him going out tonight," he said. "Watch television or something. And I mean it. No discussion. You hear me?"

"Yes, sir," I said. I was just as glad not to have to go with Jubal to the Montgomery place. And then I thought of Bessie telling me to stay out of the quarters after supper. What was she talking about?

Later that night, I was almost drifting off to sleep when I heard something. A bang. Like somebody was out in the woods hunting. It was muffled, not too close but not all that far either. But nobody would be hunting in the summer. I got out of bed and hurried to the back door and looked out the screen door into the darkness.

More bangs. It was gunfire. That was for sure. And it was coming from the direction of the quarters.

"Go back to bed," Poppa said.

I jumped. I hadn't seen him sitting alone at the kitchen table.

"What is it?" I asked.

"Go back to bed," he said again.

I went to my room and lay down. I couldn't sleep. I kept wondering what had happened, and if anyone was dead.

FOURTEEN

THE FUNERAL FOR GIDEON MONTGOMERY was
Monday afternoon at Cedar Hill Baptist Church.
Poppa was a pallbearer. Ike sat on the front row with
several of his aunts, uncles, and cousins, including
Reno and Toby and all the other McCarthys.

Afterward, while we were riding home, Poppa mentioned how much property Ike was going to inherit.
"He could quit the plant if he wanted," he said. "He
don't farm no way, and if he sold just a little of that
land, he'd have plenty to live on."

Jubal hadn't shown up to run that morning and
had to work for Mrs. Pouncey all day, so I didn't see
him until he came to the house that evening. I was
waiting for him in the backyard. He said he'd overslept
because they hardly got any sleep last night. He took
his knife out of his pocket and began cleaning his
fingernails.

"Poppa made me stay in last night," I said. "What
happened, anyway?"

He told me that two carloads of night riders raced into the quarters and kicked in the door at the Averys' house, looking for Brelove. But there wasn't anybody in the house. Mrs. Avery was staying with her sister because she knew they were coming.

"Did you see who they were?" I asked.

"We were all on the floor in the kitchen, kneeling down and praying. Then there was all that shouting and shooting. Reverend Graham says it was a real miracle of God nobody got shot." He looked at me hard. "Do *you* know who they was?"

"How should I know?" I said, indignant at the implication.

The back door opened, and Glory said, "You boys get cleaned up for supper. And remember to wipe your feets before coming inside."

Squirrel came over just as we were finishing eating. We sat on the back steps, and Jubal took out his knife.

"Tell him about last night," I said to Jubal, and he did.

"But why?" asked Squirrel. "What did Brelove do to make them so upset?"

"For a smart man, he wasn't so smart," said Jubal. "Mama says that he went up to the front door of a white lady's house. His car had broken down and he wanted to use the phone."

I agreed. That wasn't too smart.

"And something else," said Jubal. "We missed a golden opportunity today."

"What?" I asked.

"During the funeral. That's when we should have got that lumber."

"What if we got a price from the lumberyard?" said Squirrel. "We could save up for a while and—"

"Ain't no need buying what by rights is already ours," said Jubal. "Tomorrow we get it."

A bell sounded from across the road. It was Mrs. Kogan, ringing for supper. Squirrel stood up to leave, and Jubal grabbed his arm. "Tomorrow morning. We'll meet here and go get it all."

Squirrel didn't reply but pulled himself free and started walking toward the road.

"Nine o'clock," Jubal called after him.

I gave Jubal a ride on the scooter back to his house.

In the quarters, I was surprised to see a white woman sitting on Reverend Graham's front porch. Normally the only white people you saw in the quarters were men collecting rent or payments on burial insurance. There used to be a white woman who drove down in a Cadillac to pick up her maid, but, other than her, I never saw a white woman in the quarters.

There was a Negro woman with her, and I'd never seen her before, either. Both were wearing dungarees and tennis shoes and white blouses.

Jubal and I sat down on his porch and watched them. "What you reckon they doing here?" Jubal said.

In a few minutes, Glory and Alvina arrived. Glory looked at us with a puzzled expression, since we were just sitting on the porch. Then she noticed we were looking toward the reverend's house. "Who that?" she asked.

Neither of us said anything.

Alvina sauntered down the road toward Reverend Graham's.

Glory gave a little laugh. "That girl," she said. "Don't she beat all?"

We watched Alvina walk right up to the porch and talk with the two women for a few minutes. Then she came back to us. I could see the smugness in her face and knew she was dying to tell us what she'd found out.

"They're COFO workers," she said. "They going to be staying with Reverend Graham and setting up a Freedom School at the church. They both from California."

"We got enough schools around here," said Jubal.

"It's to teach people how to register to vote. That white one is Tamara and the other one is named Esther. They say they know Johnny." If they were friends of Jubal's older brother, then I knew I wasn't going to like them.

"They coming this way," said Jubal.

As they walked toward us, it occurred to me that these were the invaders folks were talking about, part of the thousands and thousands that were coming to Mississippi that summer. These were the ones Poppa said were trying to stir up trouble and get the coloreds all riled up.

The white woman wasn't very tall. She had long black hair pulled back in a ponytail. The Negro woman was tall and dark like cooking chocolate and stood very erect.

"We'd like to talk to your parents," the white woman said to Alvina, smiling.

Alvina darted into the house.

The two women stood in front of the porch, smiling and looking at us. "Do you live here?" the white one asked Jubal.

He nodded.

She didn't ask me anything.

I did notice the Negro woman was looking at me. I wasn't sure what kind of look it was.

Alvina the Fly jumped out onto the porch again.

Glory opened the screen door and took one step onto the porch and smiled at the two women. Jerome came to the doorway and leaned against the doorjamb.

The white woman said she was Tamara Feinstein and the other one was Esther Garrison. "We're from the University of California at Berkeley," she said. "Pleased to meet you." Even though Tamara was smiling, I could tell by the way her voice trembled a little that she was very nervous.

"Actually, I grew up in Alabama," Esther said. "Obadiah."

"And I'm originally from New York," said Tamara. She was talking faster and louder now. "We love Mississippi." She paused and looked at Glory and

Jerome, as if waiting for them to respond. Neither said anything. Tamara continued, talking even louder and faster. "We have come to teach people how to register to vote and about their constitutional rights as American citizens."

I noticed Jubal's mouth was sagging open. I don't think he'd ever heard anyone talk so fast in all his life. As a matter of fact, neither had I.

Esther stepped forward, closer to the edge of the porch. "We would like you all to come to the school," she said, looking up at Jerome. "Reverend Graham said you are a deacon in the church, Mr. Suddith. Your influence would be very helpful with what we are doing."

Jerome still leaned again the doorjamb. "What's it cost?" he asked.

"It's free," said Esther.

"I'm pretty tired most evenings," he said.

"It won't last that long," said Tamara.

"I don't think so," he said.

"I want to go," said Alvina.

"Sure," said Tamara. "You boys are invited too."

"I get enough of school," said Jubal.

"Can I go?" Alvina was asking Glory.

"I don't think none of us needs to go," said Jerome.

Alvina didn't acknowledge him. "Can I?" she asked Glory again.

Jerome moved away from the doorway and disappeared into the house.

"Thank you for coming by," said Glory. She went back into the house.

Tamara gave Esther a confused look.

Esther said, "Let's go. I'll tell you about it."

They left, and Alvina jumped up the front steps and ran into the house, letting the screen door bang. Jubal and I were still sitting on the edge of the porch, watching the two women stopping in front of the Tannerhills' house.

I could hear Alvina talking with Jerome.

"But why not?" she said in an exasperated voice.

"The answer is no," Glory said.

"But Johnny says everyone else will be going to the school."

"I don't want to hear any more about it. The answer is no."

"I ain't afraid," Alvina said defiantly.

She flew out of the house again, banging the screen door again, and flitted up the road to a small crowd that was gathering around Esther and Tamara.

I looked at Jubal. He was very upset about something. "What's wrong?" I asked.

"Forget it," he said, walking away from me.

FIFTEEN

THE NEXT MORNING, Mrs. Pouncey decided she needed Jubal to do some extra work, so we didn't try to get the lumber.

Then, that evening at supper, Alvina said her brother Johnny had been at Greenwood all week and had just returned with another civil rights worker. "He's a white man," she said. By her tone I could tell she meant for me to be impressed with this incredible thing.

"He's got a beard and long hair just like Jesus," said Jubal. "Maybe he's passing, too."

"Just eat your food," Glory said. "And tell us about Mrs. Pouncey. How's she doing? Been sick anymore?"

We finished supper and I went with Jubal to the quarters. I was a bit curious to see the white man myself. Jubal pointed out a battered green Dodge station wagon parked in front of old Claude Albert's house.

"He's staying with Mr. Albert," Jubal said. "His name is Ronald Ritter."

Claude Albert's wife had died last year. Nana knew her and told me there wasn't a kinder woman on the face of the earth than Estelle Albert.

We found Ronald Ritter two roads over from the Harris's place. He and Esther and Tamara were at the Wessons' house. He had a camera and was taking pictures.

"Didn't I tell you his hair was as long as Jesus'?" said Jubal. "I bet he straightens it."

Johnny Harris was there too. He grinned at Jubal when we walked up and hit his stomach with the back of his hand. "This is my football-playing brother and my beautiful baby sister," Johnny said to Ronald. He put his arm around Alvina's shoulders, and she gave a shy smile. It wasn't often that she was shy about anything.

Johnny didn't introduce me or even look at me.

Ronald Ritter stooped down slightly and took a photograph of Johnny standing with his arm around Alvina, and then he photographed me and Jubal standing together.

"It's for history," Johnny said to Alvina. "Did you know you were going to be in history now?" He gave her a squeeze and laughed.

Ritter took out a notebook. "Tell me your names," he said.

"Jubal and Alvina," Johnny said. "Harris."

"And that's Cooper," said Esther Garrison, looking down at me from the porch. I smiled back and looked down, slightly embarrassed now that everyone was staring at me.

"And last name?" Ronald said, looking at me.

I told him and he wrote it down.

"Umm. Interesting," he said, still looking at me as he backed away taking another picture of me.

I noticed that, unlike Tamara, he didn't have a Yankee accent.

Curtis Miller, a friend of Johnny's and also a college student, took a pistol out of his pocket and grinned. I didn't care for Curtis. He had beady little eyes that reminded me of a rattlesnake.

"Hey, Mr. Photographer Man," he said, grinning. "Take a picture of this."

Ritter raised his camera.

Curtis made a menacing face and pointed the pistol straight at the camera. Then he laughed.

Johnny laughed, too, and said, "Put that thing away 'fore you shoot yourself or somebody else." I noticed, however, that Johnny's tone wasn't forceful, and he was smiling. It was almost as if he enjoyed seeing Curtis brandishing the weapon.

Curtis walked over to the porch where Tamara was sitting with her legs dangling off the side. He brought his face very close to hers, smiled, and held the gun up only inches in front of her eyes and said, "You ever seen a real gun, Miss Lady from New York City?"

Tamara gave a tense smile and looked nervously toward Esther as if asking for help. Esther was scowling.

"I wouldn't be at all surprised if this here gun has killed itself a bunch of white folks," Curtis continued. He touched the side of Tamara's face with the barrel.

"That's enough," said Esther.

Curtis looked up at her and grinned. "Maybe I need to take care of you, too, Miss California College High and Mighty."

"Get that gun away from her face or I'll make you eat it," Esther said through her teeth.

Curtis laughed. "Will you now?" he said. "My, my, my. What big talk we have."

"Come on, Curtis," Johnny said. "We got to roll."

"Just a minute," Curtis replied. "I think I have been challenged."

"What's going on here?" came the deep voice of Reverend Graham. His forehead was furrowed and his jaw jutted out.

Curtis brought the pistol down to his side. "Just showing them all my new target pistol, Reverend," he said. He was looking straight at me.

"We don't need pictures of all this," Reverend Graham said to Ritter, who had been shooting his camera continuously.

"Yes, sir," said Ritter agreeably as he lowered the camera.

"Come on," Johnny said to Curtis. "Let's go."

Curtis stepped away from the porch and put the pistol in his pocket.

Johnny hooked his arm around Jubal's neck and

moved onto the road. Curtis followed, walking close to me as he did. As he passed, he whacked me with his elbow and then said, "Oh, excuse me. I didn't see you."

My lungs felt paralyzed.

I watched as Johnny and Jubal reached Johnny's car. Then Johnny gave him a good-natured shove on the shoulder and he and Curtis got into the car and drove away. One of the taillights was out.

I felt a hand on my shoulder. It was Esther. She smiled at me. Her teeth were perfectly straight and perfectly white. But it was her eyes that fixed me. They were strong. And kind. "I'm glad you're here, Cooper," she said. She squeezed my shoulder, then walked toward Tamara, who was now standing in between the two houses, staring out toward the darkness of the woods.

There was the sound of a siren from the main road.

"Sheriff car," said Jubal.

"Maybe the fire truck," I said. Poppa was on the town's volunteer fire department.

The siren stopped.

We looked at each other. It sounded like it had stopped right about where my house was.

I started the scooter, and Jubal jumped on back.

SIXTEEN

AS WE NEARED MY HOUSE, I could see the flashing red lights of the sheriff's car. It was parked across the road in the front yard of Squirrel's house. Something was burning in the yard, and several cars and pickups were parked along the road. The smell of smoke choked the air.

I stopped the scooter right at the edge of the driveway. I could see then that it was a cross burning. It was taller than a man's head and made of croker sacks, looked like, covering two-by-fours. Flames shot up into the darkness much taller than the full-grown oak tree beside the cross. I could feel the heat as Jubal and I got off the scooter.

Squirrel was standing near the house. His mother had one arm around him and one around his little brother, Jacob. Mr. Kogan was talking with the sheriff with his hands jerking all around. Uncle Chicago was standing beside Mr. Kogan with his fists on his hips, the way he always puts them when he's upset.

We walked closer to the fire.

"Who would do this?" Mr. Kogan said to the sheriff. "We've lived here twenty years and nothing like this has ever happened."

"I'm sure it was just meant to be a joke," Sheriff Skinner said.

"Joke? Are you serious?" said Uncle Chicago. "Who would joke about a thing like this?"

I wondered where the fire department was. I walked over to Poppa, who was standing beside Ike Montgomery. "How come nobody's putting it out?" I asked.

"It'll burn itself out," Poppa said. "Ain't no danger to the house."

Jubal had moved back into the shadows near the house. Squirrel had gotten away from his mother, and was beside Jubal. I went over to them.

"Who did it?" I asked.

Squirrel gave a cynical laugh. "They didn't exactly leave us a calling card or anything," he said.

Sheriff Skinner returned to his car and switched off the flashing lights.

Mr. Wrightson was now talking with Mr. Kogan. Mr. Wrightson owned the largest grocery store in town.

"Mr. Wrightson has been after Daddy to sell the store," Squirrel said. "I guess he thinks this is an opportune time to make another offer." He spit on the ground.

Mr. Kogan shook his head at Mr. Wrightson then

walked up to the cross with a shovel and pushed it over. It crashed to the ground, sending a spray of sparks flying into the air. Several pieces of burlap broke loose and started patches of the grass on fire. Ike, Poppa, and several other men stomped out the flames.

"Well?" shouted Mr. Kogan, facing the onlookers. "Are you all happy? Is this the way you treat other people? You are cowards! Cowards! Every last one of you!"

Mrs. Kogan had walked over to us. "Stay close by me," she said to Squirrel. Then she looked at us and said, "Thank you, boys, for coming." She hugged both of us.

Mr. Kogan walked toward the house, calling Mrs. Kogan and the two boys to follow him.

SEVENTEEN

THE NEXT MORNING Squirrel and Jubal were waiting
for me when I got home from Uncle Chicago's. They
were sitting in the shade of the large oak beside the
garage and stood up as I parked the scooter.

I had never seen Squirrel so upset. I was upset, too,
and had a hard time getting to sleep the night before.
All I could see in my mind was that cross burning.

"What I want to know is what are the Scorpions
going to do about this?" Squirrel asked.

The question wasn't one I had considered, and the
very thought of doing something made me extremely
uncomfortable. "What do you mean?" I asked.

"I mean, somebody has incinerated up half our
front yard." His voice was trembling with anger.

"He thinks he knows who it was," Jubal said to me.

"I don't just think. I know," said Squirrel. "It was
Reno McCarthy."

"But he wouldn't have been alone," I said.

"What do you want to do—burn a cross in his yard?" asked Jubal.

"Listen," I said to Squirrel. "I don't think you know the kind of men we're talking about. They ain't the kind that just throw rocks."

"I think you're both chicken. That's what I think," Squirrel said with a sneer. "Scorpions. What a joke."

"He's right," Jubal said to me. "We can't let anyone do this to one of our members."

"Let's think about it," I said, hating myself for sounding like such a coward. In fact, I knew I sounded a lot like Squirrel sounds most of the time.

"I'm going do something if I have to do it myself," said Squirrel.

He turned around and walked down the driveway. We watched him cross the road and head toward his house.

Later I couldn't keep my mind off what Squirrel had said. I decided we needed to talk. He was working at his father's store that afternoon, so I rode to town.

Mrs. Kogan and Jacob were there also. I think Mr. Kogan didn't like them at home alone.

Squirrel was hanging flashlights onto a rack. "What do you want?" he asked when I walked up.

"Can you come over tonight?" I asked.

"No. My father won't let me go out after supper for a while. Not that I'm scared, mind you."

"I know that," I said. Asking him that wasn't why I'd come to see him, of course. I continued, "Listen, I don't know how or when, but we're going to get even with them for what they did."

"I'll believe it when I see it," he said, not looking at me.

"I swear we will."

Mr. Kogan, wearing his blue work apron, walked over toward us. "Aaron has work to do, Cooper," he said.

"Yes, sir," I said. I left then, but didn't feel any better in spite of making that commitment to Squirrel.

When I got home, I went to my room and sat down at the table in the corner and wrote a letter. I carefully printed each word and when I was done, I wiped the sheet with a handkerchief to be sure no fingerprints were on it. It read:

Reno,
We know what you and the others did. Beware.
We will get you for this. You can be sure of that.
                              The Scorpions

I drew a picture of a scorpion with its tail arched, ready to sting.

That night, before we worked out, I told Jubal what I'd said to Squirrel and showed him the letter. He nodded when he finished reading it. "And if you mail this, we gonna have to do something." There was a cold look in his eyes. "But we'll have to wait for the right time. Right now we need to go get that lumber and tin."

"We ought to wait till Squirrel can help us," I said. "He can't go out at night for a while, he said."

"We waited long enough as it is. The stuff is rightfully ours."

I knew there was no use trying to talk Jubal out of anything he'd made up his mind about. He was mule headed that way. So was his father, Marcellus, Uncle Chicago said. He told me that when they were boys, Marcellus told him once that when he was grown he was never going to say "Sir" to another white man as long as he lived. And he didn't either, Uncle Chicago said.

Glory called us to supper.

"Eat your greens," Mama said to me at the table, "and stop playing with your food."

"Like I was saying," Nana said. "It ain't going to happen."

They had been talking about the possibility of mixing the races in the schools. A lot of people said that's what the federal government was going to do in the fall.

Nana was never in doubt about anything, whether telling what the governor was going to do or how to run R and M Trucking, where she had been office manager for almost forty years, or in instructing me how to dress. I never paid her any mind, of course.

Jubal stepped toward the doorway of the kitchen, looking at me and motioning me to finish. He was done already. I knew there wasn't any sense in not going on. Might as well go ahead and get it over with. And we needed the material to build the hideout.

"May I be excused?" I asked.

"What's the hurry?" Poppa said.

"Jubal and me got some stuff to do."

"No, I got something for you to do. Wait for me outside. We got someplace to go."

"Where?" I asked.

"Just wait outside," he said.

"Angus, he doesn't need to go," Mama said.

"Ain't going to be nothing there but white trash," Nana said. Her mouth was twisted up like it gets when she smells something dead.

"Do what I say," he said to me.

Jubal and I went outside and sat on the front steps. He was whittling on a short stick with the knife Mr. Montgomery gave him. "Where're y'all going?" he asked.

"I don't know. Maybe it won't take too long, then I'll ride over to your house and we can do it. It ain't dark for a long time."

The screen door opened and Poppa came out and stepped down around me. "Let's go," he said, walking toward the drive where the pickup was parked.

Jubal and I stood up.

"I'll—" I started to say.

"C'mon," said Poppa, opening the truck's door. It was then I noticed he had his pistol shoved down into his belt.

We drove through town and across the tracks and onto Highway 9. Poppa was driving faster than usual.

"Where're we going?" I asked.

"We got some business to take care of," he said.

The highway wound past open pastureland and long stretches of hardwoods. After at least five miles, Poppa turned onto a single-lane dirt road.

The name "Wrightson" was lettered on the dented mailbox beside the road. The lettering was not very good. The *W* looked like an upside down *M,* and the letters were more and more scrunched up as they moved to the right, indicating the letterer could see he was running out of space. I knew all about lettering because Uncle Chicago had been teaching it to me for two years. The only Wrightson I knew was Mr. Wrightson, who I'd last seen in Squirrel's front yard.

The road passed a brick house on the right and turned into a thick stand of hardwood trees before dead-ending at a pasture. At the end of the road stood two men with pump shotguns. One of the men held up his hand for us to stop.

He came to the driver's side of the car and leaned down and smiled across at me. "Glad to see you brought your boy, Angus." He patted the top of the door. "Got quite a crowd already." He stepped back and waved us on.

We followed a cow trail through the pasture up a long grade to a large cluster of cars and pickups. Poppa pulled to a stop, and we walked up to the crowd of men and boys gathered in front of a large flatbed truck. Many of the men carried guns.

At one end of the flatbed was a Confederate flag and on the other end was an American flag. A hillbilly band was playing in the center of the truck.

Several men wearing white-hooded robes with just their faces showing stood near the band. For a split second, I thought they were Catholic priests. They had red-and-purple crosses sewn on the front of their robes. But then I understood who they were, even though until that moment I had never seen any. Of course, I'd never seen any Catholic priests, either.

"They're from south Mississippi," Poppa said to me.

I had heard of the Ku Klux Klan all my life from Poppa. When he talked about the Civil War and Reconstruction days, he told how the Yankees set up the coloreds in charge. Then the Klan, Poppa said, frightened the coloreds into not voting anymore, and the white folks got back in control. The coloreds, Poppa said, thought the men in white robes were ghosts.

Guin Peoney, who worked at the plant with Poppa, greeted us. I liked Guin. He and Poppa belonged to the same deer camp, and he wasn't like a lot of the other men, always saying something foolish to me, trying to get a laugh out of the other men. Guin talked with me just like he would with Poppa. Poppa said that was because Guin was only in his twenties and wasn't really that much of a man himself.

"What do you think, Angus?" he asked.

"Don't know," said Poppa. "What do you think?"

"Don't know yet."

Ike Montgomery walked up to us but didn't say anything. A shudder trickled down my spine.

I moved slowly back a ways. He didn't nod at me in recognition when he walked up, and our eyes met only for a second or two. He had pale cloudy eyes that looked like a molting snake's.

The band began playing "Dixie" and a lot of men shouted and raised their guns over their heads. Some fired into the air.

Poppa, Guin, and Ike stood perfectly still. Ike had his arms crossed and stared toward the truck-bed stage as if he were bored.

I saw Reno McCarthy jumping around like he was getting happy at a revival. He had his .22 rifle and he fired and whooped. I wondered if he knew how silly he looked with his red hair combed in ducktails with a waterfall front. I moved to the other side of Poppa just so I wouldn't have to look at him.

The band stopped playing, and Mr. Wrightson stepped to the edge of the stage and held up his hands, for everybody to get quiet. He was a very heavy man and the sweat was soaking though his short-sleeved white shirt.

He said there was important business to be done,

and, to help them get organized, several members of the White Knights of the Ku Klux Klan of Mississippi had come up from Laurel and Hattiesburg. He introduced one man as the Grand Wizard.

The man, wearing an open-face hood and thick, horn-rimmed eyeglasses, stepped to the edge of the stage and began to speak. He mentioned about the colored man enrolling at Ole Miss that very day and said that in the North, coloreds were killing people, and now the Yankees were invading Mississippi just like they did a hundred years ago.

Only he never used the word "colored."

He used the word that Nana says is only used by common people. Uncle Chicago won't allow the word said in his presence. He said saying that word is worse than taking the Lord's name in vain because, like any parent, God hates it when people say bad stuff about his children. As I already said, Uncle Chicago always used the word "Negro" and pronounced it like "knee-grow." Most people pronounced it "niggra."

Uncle Chicago also said "Negro" was more proper than "colored," which Nana preferred. Chicago said "Negro" is Spanish and Portuguese for "black" and comes from the old dead Latin language word "Niger." He also showed Alvina and me tubes of paint with the word printed out. Ivory black—*noir d'ivoire, elfenbein-schwarz, negro de marfil, negro d'avorio.*

I don't think the Grand Wizard knew all that and probably wouldn't have been interested in having

Uncle Chicago explain it to him. What he was interested in was the invasion.

"There are ten thousand Yankee beatniks coming down here to Mississippi this summer to stir things up," he said. "But what they don't know is that ninety thousand White Knights of the Ku Klux Klan will be waiting for them!"

The Grand Wizard went on to say that communism was behind all the race mixing and if it was going to be defeated in America, it would have to be done in the South and primarily in Mississippi.

"We are enlisting only sober, intelligent, courageous, Christian, American white men who are militantly determined, God willing, to save their lives and the life of this nation. Who is willing to join us? Who is willing to fight back?"

The band broke out in "Dixie" again, and everybody was yelling and screaming and shooting and jumping around. Except Ike and Guin and Poppa.

Poppa did have a strange smile on his face. A mean smile. But Ike wasn't smiling. His face was cold. Deep cold. And Guin Peoney was frowning.

Reno came right in my face and jabbed me in the chest with his fingers. "We gonna get that friend of yours," he said. "He's gonna be buried right beside that no-good daddy of his and I mean real quick."

Reno's father, Toby, was standing behind him, grinning at us.

"What?" I said, not understanding.

"Jubal Harris," he said. "You know what I'm talking about."

Ike grabbed Reno's wrist and forced him back. His whole face seemed to darken with rage. Toby McCarthy jumped forward and pushed at Ike's shoulder. "Get your hands off my boy," he said.

Ike swung around to face Toby. "Teach your boy some manners," he said.

"You want some of me?" Toby said, raising his fists. "Let's do it now."

"You're drunk," said Ike. "Somebody better get him away from me." He looked at Reno. "And that goes for you too."

Reno gave Ike a contemptuous look, then turned to me and smiled. "Remember what I said. And you can tell him if you like." He laughed. "I wish I could be there to see him pissing in his pants."

Some men pulled both Reno and Toby away.

"Let's get out of here," Poppa said, turning toward the car.

EIGHTEEN

AS WE DROVE HOME I felt sick to my stomach.

Poppa said, "Don't worry about it. That boy is nothing but talk. He's just crazy. Like all them McCarthys. Nuts."

"But why would he say that about Jubal?"

"Who knows? They're just mean. They don't even like family. Like Ike. He and Toby are first cousins, you know."

"I know."

Poppa continued. "Maybe they don't like Jubal because he's Marcellus's son, and Marcellus was a bit crazy himself. Uppity. Sassy. He just never could keep in his place."

"Jubal has mentioned him a couple of times lately," I said. "And he hadn't since Marcellus died."

"Toby was drunk. He wouldn't have done that if he wasn't drunk." He spat out the window. "Marcellus was a good farmer, though. Always made a crop of some kind no matter how hard things got."

I thought about the Grand Wizard at Mr. Wrightson's. "That man back there," I said. "What's all this killing he was talking about?"

"There's probably a lot of people going to die this summer. And any colored kid who tries to go to a white school in this county is signing his own death warrant. They need to know that and know it good."

"He was asking people to sign up," I said, letting the statement hang out there to see what he'd say.

"Ike and Guin did," he said.

"Are you going to?"

"I'll have to think about it."

We were driving due west. The sun had already disappeared below the horizon, and the sky glowed red. I closed my eyes, kept swallowing hard and leaned my head close to the window to let the rushing air hit my face.

At the house, I jumped out the car and took a deep breath. It was already eight-thirty, and the night air was cooling down. Poppa went to check on his dogs.

I went inside and told Mama I was going to Jubal's.

"Don't be gone long," Mama said.

I rode my motor scooter over to the quarters. The dog at the house across the street from the Harris's barked fiercely as I parked, and the chickens in Jubal's front yard scurried under the house. The air was thick with the smell of cooking fires.

The front door was open and light from inside

flowed onto the porch, where Jubal sat with his legs dangling over the side. He was whittling on a stick and leaning against a leg of the wringer washer. Nana had given the washer to Glory after she got her new Maytag.

Glory was proud of that washer and, although Jerome told her it ought to go on the back porch, insisted on putting it on the front porch where everybody could see it. The washer's hose ran down off the side of the porch toward the water tap.

Jubal's house, like most homes in the quarters, was a small, board-and-batten, unpainted house with a sagging front porch. It had a front room and two tiny bedrooms and a kitchen in the rear. Each house was separated from its neighbor by a wide vegetable garden.

"Where you been?" asked Jubal. "It be too late to find rocks now."

"We were with some men from the deer camp," I said, not wanting to say anything specific about the rally. "Ike Montgomery was there, too. But he didn't say nothing to me."

Jubal spit on the ground. "I ain't interested in no Ike Montgomery."

"Do you know what a beatnik is?" I asked.

"It's a type of bug. Very poisonous."

"No, it's a person, and there's about ten thousand of them going to invade Mississippi this summer."

"Who told you that?"

"It's just what I heard."

Mocking laughter came from the darkened window on the right side of the house. It was Alvina the Fly. She had her face up to the window screen.

"What you doing listening to us?" said Jubal. "And what you doing in Mama's room in the dark anyways?"

"Beatniks live in big cities in New York and California and have beards, Chicken Coop," she said. "And I highly doubt there are ten thousand of them in the whole wide world. Probably not even five thousand. They play bongo drums."

Alvina spoke all the time like she knew she was right. She thought she was a lot smarter than either Jubal or me or, in fact, than the two of us put together, and was forever asking us questions like, Who was the ninth president? Quick, tell me. Or, How many books are there in the Bible, or How long did Moses live? Or, Who was Harriet Tubman, or What's a marsupial?

I usually just ignored her.

She left the window and a moment later popped out onto the front porch. She put her hands on her hips and said, "And it ain't beatniks who are coming. It's college students like Esther and Tamara and Ronald. Thousands of them. They're coming from all over America."

"Who told you that?" asked Jubal. He and I both were always skeptical about some of Alvina's bolder predictions.

"Johnny told me," she said, raising her chin smugly.

"Come on," Jubal said to me. "Let's walk." We moved away from the porch.

"Y'all don't know nothing," Alvina called out. "What's the Civil Rights Bill? Come on. Somebody tell me. What does it mean?"

We kept walking away.

"I'll tell you what it means," she said. "It means I'm going to the white school this year, Cooper Grant. That's what it means."

Jubal whirled around and said to her, "Shut your face, girl. You know Mama ain't letting you do no such thing."

She laughed and went back into the house.

I couldn't stop thinking about what Reno said to me about Jubal. "I know why I can't stand Reno McCarthy, and I know why Squirrel don't like him," I said. "How come you don't like him?"

"He's a toad, and I ain't scared of him or his father."

"How do you know them?"

Jubal was slow in answering. "Mr. McCarthy was all the time hassling Daddy," he said.

"But what's that got to do with you?"

"Me and Reno, we had a run-in in town one time. He said something to me in front of some other boys, and I should have beat the crap out of him then and there, but I didn't. I just ignored him and kept on walking. He started yelling after me and called me a name."

I didn't have to ask what name. "Are you sure there ain't more to it than that?"

"You mailed that letter yet?" he asked.

"I'm going to do it tomorrow."

He smiled. "Good. Very good. What kind of noise do Scorpions make?"

"I think they hiss like a snake."

He made a hissing sound, then laughed. "I wish I could see Reno when he reads that letter." He hissed again.

NINETEEN

THE NEXT DAY was Saturday. I went to town after lunch and put the letter in the slot at the post office.

In the afternoon, Poppa told me there was a meeting at Wrightson's store, and he wanted me to go with him. Wrightson's grocery store was in downtown Chulosa on Court Street. Poppa parked on the street, and we went around the side of the building to the loading dock.

There was a man with a straw hat pulled down almost to his eyes standing in front of the door. He spit tobacco juice to the side, then grinned at us. "This your boy, Angus?" he asked.

"Cooper, this is Moses Jackson," Poppa said.

Mr. Jackson and I shook hands. His hand was so callused that it felt like pieces of rock.

"Nice looking young man," he said, opening the door for us.

We walked into the store's storage room. Shelves of foodstuffs and other goods lined the walls. On wooden pallets in the middle of the room were large sacks of flour and sugar.

Several men stood around talking and smoking. One man took a drink from a bottle and passed it around. The bottle had no label, and I wondered if it was one Jubal and I had sold back to Mr. Strickland.

Tom Jackson was there. He played on the football team and, like me, was third team last year. I assumed it was his father I'd met at the door. We nodded at each other.

Reno McCarthy and his father were on one side laughing with two other men. Reno looked up when we walked in, and sneered.

Bobby Mac Simmons was also there. Bobby Mac started at halfback. He gave me a wave.

Russell Wrightson walked up to us and shook hands with Poppa and then with me. "Well, now, Angus," he said. "I'm glad you got this boy down here finally. And the next thing I need to do is to get him in my Sunday school class." He looked down at me, grinning wide so that I could see how cigarette stained his teeth were.

Coach Bill Turner entered the room and called out a general greeting to everyone in his loud voice. He saw me and immediately walked up and slapped me on the back. "You in shape, son?" he asked. "You know it's only four weeks till we start two-a-days?" He nudged my stomach with the back of his fist. "It sure is good to see you here. Yes, indeed."

"We need to get started," Mr. Wrightson called out.

Everyone got quiet.

Casey Donald and Guin Peoney stood next to Poppa. And, in a corner by himself, I saw Ike Montgomery. He was as still as a statue except for those pale, cold eyes, which moved slowly from one person to another. When he looked at me, I looked away.

"I thought it would be good to get back together and see how things are going," said Mr. Wrightson. "I don't know any more about what's happened to these race-mixers who disappeared down at Philadelphia than you do. I think it's a hoax myself. It's just something the NAACP dreamed up to get the federal government all upset."

All week long the *Daily Journal* had been full of stories about their disappearance, and how the National Association for the Advancement of Colored People and other COFO groups were saying they were probably dead, and how hundreds of FBI men were flying into the state to look for them. Poppa said they had sneaked back up North and just wanted everyone to think they were dead so Mississippi would look bad.

"Even if those boys have got themselves killed," Mr. Wrightson continued, "what did they expect coming down here where they don't belong?"

Several men grunted agreements.

"What about these Freedom Schools?" a man asked. "I've heard we got some of these COFO people right here in town. What are we going to do about it?"

"That's right," Mr. Wrightson said. "There're two of them from California. A colored gal and a Jew woman. They're living with the colored preacher in the quarters."

He obviously didn't know about Ronald Ritter. But how did he know where Esther and Tamara were staying?

"The longer they remain here the more they are going to stir up the coloreds," said Toby McCarthy. "Something needs to be done. That preacher might need a visit some night, and I mean real soon."

"That's right," said another man. "It's like a cancer. The quicker you deal with it, the better."

Others agreed.

Mr. Wrightson held up his hands for quiet. "Listen, now," he said. "Everything that needs to be done will be done, everything in its proper time. We know what they are doing. And we'll be ready for each move they make."

"One of them is already getting out of hand," Reno said loudly.

Everybody turned to look at him.

He was looking at me. "I'm talking about Jubal Harris," he said.

"What do you mean?" asked Poppa.

"He don't know his place."

I clenched my hands into fists. "You stuck a gun in his face for no reason," I said.

"Hold it, hold it," said Mr. Wrightson. "We can't

go around chasing small fish right now. We have to concentrate on the bigger ones. Now a lot of us got good Negro friends just like Cooper here has. There's nothing wrong with that. It's the ones that are getting riled up that we need to be aware of. And, you believe me on this . . ." He paused and looked around at each person to be sure they were paying attention. "There ain't one blessed thing that they are doing or even *thinking* about doing but that I don't know about it. Do I have to say any more?"

He waited for a response. No one said anything.

"So," said Mr. Wrightson. "Some things are in the works. That's what I wanted you to know. We ain't just sitting on our butts doing nothing."

On the way home, Poppa asked me to explain about Reno sticking a gun in Jubal's face. I did.

"What was Jubal supposed to do?" I said. "Let that fool blow his brains out?"

"Reno is crazy," Poppa said. "You stay out of his way."

We rode on through town and passed the turnoff to the quarters and turned onto the road leading to home.

"Tell me about Ike Montgomery," I asked.

"Ike? Well, he was in sausage with me at the plant for a while but now he's in bologna with Casey. But I expect he's gonna quit now that he's got his daddy's land and all."

"Nana said he was a friend of Uncle Chicago's growing up."

"Yes, he and Chicago were always big buddies. But they were a little older than me so I didn't know them that well."

"And Marcellus Harris."

"He and Ike was probably like you and Jubal. Liked to do things together, and that's okay."

"I can't believe he hanged himself."

Poppa pulled into our drive and parked under the trees on the side of the house. "He was drunk," he said, opening his door. "Go on inside. I need to go out and check on the dogs."

I rode over to Uncle Chicago's and told him about the meeting at Wrightson's Grocery Store.

He wiped his brush and looked at me. "And?" he asked slowly.

"Mr. Wrightson said they were going to do some things," I said.

"What things?"

"He didn't say."

He leaned back in his chair. "Who all was there?"

I told him. He didn't seem surprised by any name, not even his friend Ike Montgomery.

I hadn't told Uncle Chicago about us finding Mr. Montgomery, or that we were planning to get the tin and lumber that, as Jubal said, was due us, or that the thought on going back onto that property and maybe running into Ike kept gnawing at me. But I was also curious to know more about this man with eyes like a snake's.

"What happened to Marcellus and Ike?" I asked.

"Nothing."

"They had an argument, according to Jubal."

"Marcellus was like a brother to Ike."

"Then how can he be in the Klan?"

"It's not always easy to understand why he does the things he does." He looked at his watch. "I've got to go to Tupelo," he said.

"One more thing," I said. "Mr. Wrightson said he knows everything they're planning."

Uncle Chicago cocked his head. "He said that?"

"Yes, sir."

He rubbed his forehead for a moment, then said, "We'll have to think on that."

He looked at his watch. "I have to go," he said.

I went back outside.

TWENTY

SUNDAY MORNING, Bessie picked me up, running late as usual. When we arrived at the church and got out of the car, I saw Jerome and Mr. Cunningham kneeling down, looking under the church. They both got up as we approached, brushed off their knees, and greeted us.

After we entered our classroom, I looked out the window again. The two deacons had moved further down the side of the church, both on their knees again, looking under the building. Bessie caught my eye and shook her head. I understood I wasn't to say anything about what I'd seen.

During the worship hour, Reverend Graham had both Tamara Feinstein and Esther Garrison rise and come to the speaker's stand beside the piano and tell who they were and why they had come to Mississippi all the way from California.

Tamara said that her family lived on Central Park West in New York City now but that her father had been in a concentration camp in Germany when he was young and that her family had always felt very passionately about people who were oppressed because of their religion or race. She and Esther were friends at Berkeley, and when a man from the Student Nonviolent Coordinating Committee came to their campus last February and told about the Mississippi Project, they knew they had to come and help.

Then Esther stood at the speaker's stand. She told about growing up in Obadiah, Alabama, and how, when she was a girl, a white man shot and killed her father for drinking out of the same dipper the man's family used. She said nothing was ever done to the white man for murdering her father.

All during the rest of service I couldn't stop looking at Esther. She had her head slightly bowed, and she didn't sing when the congregation did or make any visible reaction to Reverend Graham's sermon.

After church, Jubal had to talk with Sister Adams about some work she wanted him to do, and I stood at the side of the building in the shade, waiting for Bessie. She was usually one of the last ones to leave the building. It seemed like she had to shake hands with every single person there.

Johnny Harris and Curtis Miller were laughing about something as they came down the front steps. Johnny noticed me and said something to Curtis. They walked over to me, mean smiles on their faces. Curtis stood on one side of me and Johnny on the other, and they pressed in close, looking down at me, still smiling.

"Don't you know this is a Negro church," Curtis said. "You got to have African blood to be a member here. You got any African blood?"

I could feel my heart racing. "I . . . I'm a baptized member—"

"You ain't nothing but white," said Johnny. "And the time is coming for all white people to leave."

"Is there a problem here?" came the strong voice of Esther. I hadn't seen her and Tamara walk up.

Curtis and Johnny moved slightly away from me. Then Johnny gave a derisive laugh and walked away. "C'mon, Curtis," he said.

Curtis stopped in front of Esther and held his index finger up in front of her face. "Some day . . . soon," he said. Then he sauntered after Johnny.

"You all right?" Esther asked me.

"What's going on?" asked Tamara.

"Nothing," said Esther.

Bessie was out the front door and waved for me to follow her.

On the way home, I didn't say anything about Johnny and Curtis, but I did ask her why the two deacons were looking under the church.

"Dynamite," she said. "But they were supposed to check before everyone got there. There was a mix-up. I told Reverend Graham that just wouldn't do. The church must be checked *before* everyone arrives."

TWENTY-ONE

MONDAY MORNING, Jubal insisted we get started
getting the lumber from the cabins. Squirrel went
with us.

"Maybe I should stand guard in case Ike comes,"
he said.

"He's at work," said Jubal.

"Poppa says he don't have to work anymore," I said.

"Did he say he'd quit?"

"No."

"Then he's at work," Jubal said firmly.

With our crowbars and hammers, Jubal and I started
pulling the planks from the cabin Mr. Montgomery
had indicated as the one we could use. It was already
mostly collapsed. We stacked the boards in front of the
cabin in the knee-high weeds. Squirrel's job was to pull
out the rusty nails with the claw of his hammer.

I kept glancing up the hillside in the direction of
the house where Ike Montgomery now lived alone. As
the morning wore on, the sun was scorching and sweat

boiled out all over my body. It ran into my eyes and stung.

We didn't talk. There was no sound except the loud creaks of boards being pulled loose from the studs, and Squirrel's tapping of nails out far enough to get the claw of his hammer under the heads.

I was wrestling with a particularly large board, pulling it, and saw Jubal out of the corner of my eye. He'd stopped working and was standing up, looking at something behind us.

"What?" I asked, turning around.

My heart froze.

Directly behind me, only a few feet away, stood Ike Montgomery. He had a shotgun in his hands.

"Explain yourselves," he said, not loud or soft either, but in a natural tone.

Jubal stood up straight and looked Ike square in the eye. "Mr. Gideon said we could have some boards and tin," he said.

"What for?"

I noticed his finger and thumb were switching the shotgun's safety off and on, off and on, just the way I do sometimes when I'm deer hunting and I hear the dogs running something.

"We're building a clubhouse in the woods," said Jubal.

Ike looked at me, then at Squirrel, who gave a little smile, then back at Jubal. "And whose property is this clubhouse on?"

"Ours," I said quickly, as firmly as I could.

Ike was silent for a bit, then said, "And he said, just like that, you could have this stuff?"

"He wanted us to take him someplace," Jubal said. "And when we come to get him he was . . . he was . . ."

"He wanted some biscuits," Squirrel said.

Ike turned and looked toward the cabin where we'd found Mr. Montgomery lying in bed, holding a bunch of flowers on his chest, and wearing a tie. "I see," he said, still looking at the cabin.

Then he turned and looked at me and Squirrel again, then at Jubal. "Okay," he said. "But just from this house. Don't take nothing from any others. Is that understood?"

"Yes, sir," we all three said at once.

He turned, laid his shotgun over his shoulder, and walked up the hillside.

We looked at each other wide eyed but said not a word till Ike disappeared over the crest of the hill.

"Wow!" said Squirrel. "Wowee! Can you believe that?"

"Hush," I said, giggling. "He can hear us."

"Don't make no matter what he hears," said Jubal. "This stuff is ours. We bargained for it and was ready to keep our end. Ain't our fault he died." He took the crow bar, slipped the end under a board on a side wall, and pushed hard.

It took us two days to get all the lumber pried loose, de-nailed, and dragged across the field and through the woods to the site. The strips of tin were awkward to carry, but we managed to get eight sections, the number Squirrel figured we needed, to the site.

Construction itself went quickly. We worked most of the day Wednesday, Thursday, and Friday, and pronounced it done. There was a small table and four chairs, one broken slightly, in the cabin, and Jubal insisted Ike meant we could take whatever we needed from that cabin. We arranged everything orderly and still had room to make three pine-straw-filled sleeping areas, one for each of us.

I suggested we camp out in the hideout Saturday night, and it was agreed, though Squirrel wasn't sure his parents would let him. I was to make a sign that read, "Scorpions' Lair. KEEP OUT!!!"

"What about those death-defying adventures y'all were talking about?" asked Squirrel.

"You'll see," said Jubal. "Just wait."

"I've got one I would like to suggest," said Squirrel.

Neither Jubal nor I had to ask him what it was.

Saturday morning Uncle Chicago had Alvina and me paint a still life in oil—a plate from one of his trips to Mexico, with two bananas, three apples, and a bunch of grapes.

"Whoever does the best job gets to eat the deep purple grapes," he challenged. He and Bessie were over on the couch, having coffee and talking about something the state legislators were doing.

I had my painting blocked in with thin turpentine washes. I noticed Alvina was wiping over her canvas with a rag. That meant she was starting over. I smiled. She was struggling. The grapes were going to be mine, but more importantly, I was going to beat her.

Alvina frowned and held her brush over her painting as if hesitant to put the paint down. I had never seen her so indecisive.

I smiled. "Don't those grapes look good?" I said. "Nothing like cool, sweet grapes on a hot summer morning."

Alvina turned to look at me. "Some things are a lot more important than stuffing your fat stomach, Chicken Coop," she said.

"I ain't fat, Fly."

"Your head is." She smiled as she looked back at the canvas.

I began painting impasto, not thinking what I was doing but wondering about how I could cut her down to size, but nothing came to mind. It never did fast enough. I fretted, knowing that two hours later, after class was over and she was gone, I would think of something really good.

Alvina cleaned her brushes with turpentine and began scraping her palette.

"What?" Uncle Chicago said, looking over from the couch.

"I have to go early, Mr. James," she said.

"Where're you off to, child?" asked Bessie. "Don't you be wasting Mr. James's time."

"I just have to go."

Uncle Chicago set down his coffee cup and walked over to her easel. "Okay," he said, looking at it. "But, you've not developed it enough to win the grapes, you know."

"Maybe another day," she said, smirking at me. She finished putting her gear into her paint box and stored it on the shelf. "Oh, I almost forgot," she said to me. "Jubal said to tell you he ain't going to the movies this afternoon."

"Why?" I asked.

There was a strange, excited glow in her eyes, as if telling me this was very satisfying to her. "He just ain't going," she said.

She skipped out the front door and away.

I looked at Uncle Chicago. He shrugged his shoulders and returned to the couch. "More coffee?" he asked Bessie.

TWENTY-TWO

ALTHOUGH I DIDN'T LET ON to Alvina, it did
bother me about Jubal not going to the movies. We
went to the Palace Theater almost every Saturday.
We'd stop at a pine thicket just before we got to town
so Jubal could pee, because there wasn't a rest room
for coloreds at the Palace, and Jubal said it ruined the
movie if you had to go and couldn't and had to hold it
for a couple of hours. Once we got to the theater, I'd
buy my ticket at the front and go in to sit downstairs,
and Jubal would buy his ticket at the side door and go
up to the colored section in the balcony.

I rode my scooter over to Jubal's house right after
art.

"I just don't feel like it," he said through the screen
door.

"You sick?" I asked.

"No," he said. "Maybe. I just don't feel like it."

I went home. Mama made pineapple and cheese
sandwiches for me and Missy.

"A lady at camp was asking about you," Missy said at the table. "She wanted to know why you didn't come to church."

"I go to church," I said. "Didn't you tell her that?"

Missy took a swallow of milk. "What was I supposed to tell her?"

"I'm a baptized member of Oak Grove Baptist," I said. "Just tell people that."

"I don't think so," she said.

"That's enough, Missy," Mama said, standing at the edge of the table. She looked down at me and smiled. "Someday Cooper will probably decide he doesn't want to go there. But it's okay for now."

I went on to the movie by myself. I parked the scooter on the side street and walked around to the front.

There was a line of several people at the box office, waiting to buy tickets. I saw Tamara Feinstein. She was alone and second in line. The man ahead of her moved away and went through the heavy glass door into the lobby.

Tamara bought her ticket, but instead of going through the door like I expected, she turned the opposite way and started toward the street. I noticed she had a string of tickets in her hand.

The doors of two cars parked at the curb opened, and people got out. Alvina, Esther Garrison, Johnny Harris, and Curtis Miller were with them, plus two other Negro men I didn't know. Tamara quickly tore off a ticket for each of them.

The woman in front of me said to the child with her, "Let's go, Cheryl. There's going to be trouble."

Curtis led the way up to the glass door and pushed it open.

"You can't come in here," said the man just inside the door taking tickets. "Go around to the side."

"I have a ticket," Curtis said. "You have sold me a ticket for this movie, and I have a right to sit anywhere I want."

"Ruth!" the man called to the woman in the box office. "Phone the sheriff!"

The sound of tires braking to a stop caused everyone to look. A car and a pickup had stopped in the middle of the street, and men with ax handles jumped out and ran toward us. It was Mr. Wrightson and Reno and Toby McCarthy and Casey Donald and Moses Jackson.

They ringed out around the seven people trying to get into the movie. Johnny Harris pulled Alvina behind him.

Curtis Miller stepped back out through the door and said, "We have a right—"

Moses Jackson swung his ax handle and hit Curtis on the side of his head. Curtis staggered backward and collapsed to the ground. Blood poured from the wound.

"Who else wants to open their mouth?" asked Mr. Wrightson.

"What seems to be the problem?" demanded a gravelly voice. Sheriff Francis Skinner and three uniformed deputies pushed their way to the center. Sheriff Skinner stood looking down at Curtis.

Tamara Feinstein stepped forward. "That man just hit him," she said, pointing her finger at Moses Jackson.

"Don't point at me, woman," Jackson snapped at her, "or I'll smash your ugly face."

"Let's all just calm down," said Sheriff Skinner. "Now I think you all have caused enough trouble for one day." He was talking to Tamara and the others. "Go on home now."

"You mean you aren't going to arrest him?" said Tamara, almost yelling. She was right in the sheriff's face.

"Back off, lady," he said. "Or I'll take you in for disturbing the peace."

"What about them?" She raised her finger again.

Moses Jackson jumped forward and shoved her hard in the face. She fell back against the others. Sheriff Skinner threw up his arm to block Jackson from coming after her.

Esther grabbed Tamara to keep her from falling. "Why don't you do something?" she yelled at the sheriff.

Sheriff Skinner turned to his deputies. "Arrest

these women," he said, "And hit them on the head if they give the slightest resistance."

The deputies moved in quickly and put handcuffs on both Tamara and Esther and led them away.

"Now the rest of you get out of here," the sheriff said.

Johnny Harris helped Curtis to his feet and pressed a handkerchief to the side of his head. They went to their cars.

As they passed, Alvina looked at me. She looked at me as if she were looking right through me, just like she didn't see me at all.

TWENTY-THREE

"LISTEN, HAROLD," Uncle Chicago said into the telephone receiver. "They can't be left in jail. Look what happened to those fellows down in Philadelphia." He was talking to an attorney friend of his named Harold Grayson. "Okay, okay," Uncle Chicago said. "I don't care what the bond is, we'll get it up. Let me know."

He hung up the phone and looked at me and read my thoughts. "You couldn't have done anything, you know," he said.

"It took me by surprise," I said.

"What do you think you could have done? Rushed those Klansmen? They would have knocked you silly and then who would have come to me?" He placed his hand on my shoulder. "You're okay, kid. Now, come with me."

Uncle Chicago's 1939 Chevy sounded like a tank but still got him wherever he needed to go. We drove to the quarters.

The sky was becoming very dark and the air smelled like rain. A large crowd of people was standing in front of Reverend Graham's house. Some of the women were crying, and Uncle Hosea was crying too. Others had scowls on their faces. I saw Ronald Ritter moving around taking photographs. Everyone turned to look at us as we walked up.

"I've gotten hold of an attorney," Uncle Chicago announced. "He's on his way to the sheriff's office right now. He'll take care of it."

Curtis Miller was sitting on the edge of the porch. His head was bandaged, and he looked like he was in a fog.

"Listen to me!" said Johnny Harris. "We had no more got our tickets than those men came after us. They *knew* we were coming." He was looking right at me. I felt very uncomfortable.

"I have something I want to say," came the deep voice of Reverend Graham. He was standing on the edge of his porch. "It was terrible this afternoon, but all this is going to change. Believe me. But we must remember that our primary objective this summer is not going through the front door at the picture show. Our main objective is getting registered to vote."

Johnny scowled but didn't reply.

"Big car coming," someone called out.

A gleaming cream-colored Lincoln Continental was rolling down the lane. The car stopped and the driver got out. It was Uncle Chicago's friend Harold

Grayson. He was smiling. "I have two young ladies here with me," he said.

The passenger door opened, and Tamara and Esther got out. Several people rushed forward to embrace them.

Harold Grayson walked up to Uncle Chicago. "The sheriff said he wasn't going to charge them . . . this time," he said.

"I owe you," said Uncle Chicago, shaking his hand.

Mr. Grayson punched him on the shoulder lightly and smiled. "And don't forget it, my friend."

Ronald Ritter knelt down in front of Mr. Grayson, Uncle Chicago, and me to take a picture. Mr. Grayson held up his hand in front of the lens. "Take my picture and I'll make you eat that camera," he said.

Ritter stood up and smiled. "Sorry," he said.

Mr. Grayson left, and Ritter introduced himself to Uncle Chicago. "I'm a great admirer of your work, Mr. Harrington," he said. "I saw one of your shows in New York." Ronald was almost as tall as Uncle Chicago but not nearly as broad through the shoulders.

Reverend Graham walked over and shook hands with Uncle Chicago and spoke to Bessie. He raised his eyebrows as he looked at her as if asking a silent question.

"No, nothing yet," she said.

Alvina walked up beside Bessie. "I was there, Miss Bessie," she said.

Bessie smiled down at her and gave her a hug.

"I know you were, child," she said. "And I'm proud of you."

I walked over to where Jubal was standing with some other boys. His arms were crossed and he didn't look happy. I stood there without saying anything.

Finally, Jubal spoke. "Are we still going camping tonight?"

"Sure," I said. I had completely forgotten about our plans.

"Why don't we go run a trotline?" he said. "I'll be over after supper."

"Cooper!" Uncle Chicago called. "We're leaving." He was walking back toward the car.

Alvina stepped in front of me. "I saw you there," she said. Her tone was accusatory.

I didn't say anything but hurried on after Uncle Chicago.

The wind was picking up. Heavy drops of rain splattered on the windshield as we drove away.

Uncle Chicago looked through the rearview mirror. "There's something about that fellow with the camera," he said. "Keep your eye on him."

"Why?"

"I don't know," he said, shifting gears. "A feeling. That's all."

TWENTY-FOUR

THE RAIN STOPPED as quickly as it had started. By the time supper was over, the clouds had swept on to the south and the first stars were out.

The rain also soaked the ground behind the barn and brought night crawlers up to the surface for air. I gathered a canful and had just finished checking the rigging on the cane poles when Jubal arrived. He had a bedroll slung over his shoulder and a paper sack.

"Where's Squirrel?" he asked.

I told him that I'd phoned Squirrel to see if he was going. He said his father still didn't want him going out at night for a while.

"The creek will probably be high and muddy," I said, to remind Jubal fishing may not be too good.

"Mud cats go by smell, not by sight," he said, gathering up the poles. I carried my bedroll, an acetylene torch, a small canvas tarp, and the worms.

We hiked to the hideout, left our camping gear, and

went to Hazard's Branch. We always set out our trot-line beside the bridge on the road to Uncle Chicago's place. The water was deep there and was a favorite bed for catfish.

It was full dark by the time we got to the bridge, and our shoes were caked in mud. I pumped up the torch and lit it, and we baited the hooks, lobbed the lines into the black water, and shoved the butts of the poles into the bank. When all the poles were set, I spread out the tarp and extinguished the torch. We would wait half an hour to check the lines.

We sat in silence for a while, listening to the sounds of tree frogs and crickets and other creatures of the night woods. Then he said, "I should have gone with them."

"What?"

"To the movie."

"I don't see what the big deal is about," I said. "Is it because there ain't no bathroom upstairs?"

He didn't answer my question. Instead, he said, "Auntie Selena say they gonna come burn down the whole quarters."

I licked my lips. I wanted to say *that's ridiculous,* but I knew it wasn't.

A dog barked somewhere way off.

"If it ain't the bathroom, what is it?"

"You wouldn't understand."

"Yes, I would. Tell me."

Jubal didn't answer for a moment. Then he said softly, "Whenever you have to go through a back door anywheres, it tells you something about yourself."

"What?"

He didn't answer.

There was one question that had been pinching me for a long time. I didn't know any other way to approach it than to just come right out with it. "How do you know your daddy didn't do it?" I asked.

He took a couple of slow breaths, then said, "I just know."

"Then who did it?"

"I have a good idea."

"You don't know," I challenged.

"I can tell you two. Reno McCarthy's father and . . . and Ike Montgomery."

"Ike Montgomery?" I asked, unable to believe that. "But he was your father's friend."

"*Was*," emphasized Jubal. "But then he went against Daddy."

We heard the sound of a car coming from the direction of Uncle Chicago's. The road was a dead end at Uncle Chicago's, so I assumed it must be him. I stood up and climbed the bank. But as the car got closer, I knew it didn't sound like his car. I froze instead of stepping out onto the road.

The car slowed down as it neared the bridge. The driver struck a match and lit a cigarette. Just as the car was passing, he looked out the window at me and frowned as he tossed out the match. Then he was gone.

My knees were jelly. I gave a moan.

"What? What?" said Jubal, running up the bank behind me.

"That was . . . that was Ike Montgomery . . ." I gasped, stepping into middle of the road. "He was coming from Uncle Chicago's."

I looked across the bridge and into the darkness that swallowed up the road.

"What are you doing?" Jubal called after me.

I was running down the road.

"What about the poles?"

"Leave them!" I yelled and ran as hard as I could.

Jubal quickly caught up with me and we sloshed on through the muck. I fell down twice and Jubal stopped and grabbed my hand and jerked me to my feet and on we went.

The porch light was on at the house when we reached the yard. Both of us were gasping for breath. Uncle Chicago stepped out onto the porch and closed the door behind him. He was walking down the front steps when he noticed us. He looked surprised and smiled.

"What in the world?" he said. "You're covered with mud, Cooper Grant. What are y'all doing here?"

"We saw . . . we saw Ike Montgomery . . ." I said.

"Ike's an old friend," he said, "and he just dropped by to give me a friendly warning." He looked down at my muddy pants again. "I have to go. Y'all want a ride back to the house? I could spread some newspapers on the backseat."

"No, sir," I said. "We're camping out."

"I've got to hurry," he said. He got into his car and started the engine. It sputtered and popped a time or two, then whined as he pressed the accelerator.

Jubal and I watched his red taillights until they vanished around the first curve.

"Mr. James is friends with Ike Montgomery?" Jubal asked.

"They were friends when they were boys," I said, starting back up the road. "Just like they were friends with your daddy, too."

Jubal said nothing. In the darkness I couldn't see his face. I had no idea what he was thinking.

TWENTY-FIVE

WE CAUGHT THIRTEEN CATFISH that night, and in the morning, after a breakfast of bacon and eggs cooked on a campfire in front of the hideout, we packed our gear, pulled the two stringers of catfish out of the creek, and went home.

It was Sunday and Nana's birthday. I gave her a box of chocolate-covered cherries, one of her favorite candies. I'd bought it at Ben Franklin two weeks before, wrapped it with some tissue paper Mama gave me, and hid it in my closet until that morning.

"You always ask me that," Nana said with a chuckle after I asked how old she was. "And my answer is still 'sweet sixteen and never been kissed.'" Then she laughed and her stomach shook. She gave me a big hug and squeezed me against her bosoms.

Mama said we'd have Nana's birthday cake after dinner.

"If Cooper isn't home in time, why can't we just eat

it without him?" Missy asked with a cross look. "His church takes forever to get out."

First Baptist was over promptly at twelve, and Missy was home by twelve-fifteen. That's when the family ate dinner. Mama kept mine in the oven till I got home, which was usually over an hour later.

A horn sounded outside, and Missy grabbed her Bible. "And I don't know *why* he has to go there anyway," she said, running toward the front door. "It's embarrassing when people say, 'Where does your brother go to church?'" She let the screen slam behind her.

Bessie wouldn't get to the house for at least fifteen more minutes.

"She may be onto something," Nana said to me.

I looked at her.

"You know how I feel about Bessie," she said.

And I did. She'd once told me she used to think of Bessie as her little sister when Bessie's mother, Auntie Victoria, cooked for Nana's mother.

"And I appreciate her taking you to church all these years," she continued, "but you're getting more grown-up now. Soon you'll be a man."

"Cooper, it's just that things aren't like they used to be," Mama said.

I heard Bessie's car stop in front of the house. She was unusually early. "That's my church," I said. "And I ain't going nowhere else."

"We'll talk about it later," Mama said.

I hurried outside.

"Let's move!" Bessie said as I hopped into the car. I could hear an urgency in her voice, and she didn't laugh and joke with me like she usually did riding to church, and twice she glanced at her watch.

The roads were still muddy and once, going through a curve just on the other side of the Taylor community, the rear end of the car almost sideswiped a mailbox on the side of the road.

I clutched the dashboard with both hands and felt my heart in my throat. At least, if I was going to have to die, I would die on the way to church, which ought to count for something with the Lord.

Once we arrived at church, Bessie said to me, "I have to see Reverend Graham for a minute. Go on to class and tell them I'll be there directly."

Alvina was wearing a dress with pink flowers all over it. "They was the meanest men I ever saw in my life," she was saying when I walked into the room. She was talking with the girls on their side of the room.

I sat down on the boys' side by Jubal.

"Mama skinned all those catfish last night and she say she gonna fry 'em this evening and to ask you if you want to come over," he said.

The very thought made me hungry. Nobody cooked better catfish with hushpuppies than Glory.

Bessie swept into the room all smiles. "Now," she said, sitting down at the small teacher's table. "Who can say their memory verse?"

Alvina's hand shot up before any of the other girls.

She was showing out as usual. None of us boys raised our hands. I looked out the window and wondered if the deacons had remembered to check under the church already.

During the worship hour, Reverend Graham preached about how the wicked Pharaoh forced the children of Israel to make bricks without straw and about how Moses came and told Pharaoh to let the people go but he wouldn't so the frogs and lice and flies all came in and everybody got boils and pestilence. And finally the Death Angel passed through the land, smiting all the firstborn cattle and children and there was a great cry in Egypt.

"But he passed over the houses of the children of Israel!" he shouted. "He passed over because they had the blood of the lambs smeared on their doors."

Half the congregation was standing up. Several people were waving their hands. One old woman was starting to dance in the center aisle.

"And that Death Angel is coming tonight," Reverend Graham said, his voice descending like it was sliding down a hillside. He paused and stepped off the podium and onto the floor. "Coming tonight for someone," he said, his eyes roaming the congregation.

A woman gasped loudly, and everyone became quiet. An usher in a white dress helped the old woman in the center aisle to her seat.

Some of those standing sat down. Others just remained still.

"Yes," said the pastor, walking very slowly up the aisle, "he be coming this way and going down to the quarters, looking for somebody." He paused, then said in a firm voice, "But!" He smiled. "We have a word from another angel of the Lord. The angel Gabriel."

He stopped at a pew and raised his hand with his index finger pointing and roaming down the pew from person to person until his finger was pointing straight at Curtis Miller. "Gabriel say death is in the air for one young man, and that man better get while the getting is good. Now!"

Curtis was looking at the preacher and everybody else was looking at Curtis. His head was still bandaged, and he gave a contemptuous smile but said nothing.

"Let us praise the Lord," Reverend Graham said as he returned to the pulpit. The piano started a hymn and the choir hummed first, then sang. The people clapped and sang with the choir. And Curtis sat still in his pew with his arms folded and his eyes looking defiantly at the pastor.

When church was over and we were all outside, I heard Curtis saying to Johnny Harris, "He don't scare me none. I ain't running from them. I ain't scared."

I stood near a couple of old women. I figured that if Curtis and Johnny noticed me, they wouldn't try anything with adults close by.

"Cooper, I want to thank you," someone said behind me. It was Esther Garrison.

"Ma'am?" I said.

"Don't 'ma'am' me," she said with a laugh. "That makes me feel old. No, there's no telling what might have happened if Mr. Grayson hadn't gotten to the jail so quickly."

"Uncle Chicago got him."

"But you got your Uncle Chicago." Esther gave me a wink and walked away just as Bessie came up.

Going home, Bessie drove slower, and she was humming the hymn "When All God's People Get Together."

"Tell me about the angel Gabriel," I asked.

"What's to tell?" she said with a shrug.

"It's a man, ain't it?"

She gave me a little smile. "Gabriel is from God," she said. We were passing the mailbox she almost hit on the way to church. "I think we set a record for us getting to the church house this morning, don't you?"

After dinner, Mama brought in the cake with one candle, and we sang happy birthday to Nana. It was chocolate, her favorite.

"And as a special treat to me on my birthday, I want to take my two favorite grandchildren to the picture show," Nana said as we ate the cake. Both Missy and I grinned.

The three of us went to the Palace for the three o'clock showing of *The Bridge on the River Kwai.* I noticed the blood on the sidewalk had been hosed off.

Nana said, while she normally didn't like to go to the movies on Sunday, since it was her birthday she deserved it.

Just as the movie was over, I went into the men's rest room to pee. Guin Peoney was at the sink washing his hands. I hadn't seen him since the Klan rally. He grinned at me.

"I saw you here when those Negroes tried to come in," he said.

"I was just in line."

"Of course," he said with a strange smile on his face. Then he left. I thought how odd it was the way he'd said "Negro." He'd pronounced it just like Uncle Chicago did.

Jubal came over late in the afternoon. We sat on the back porch. He was whittling on a small piece of hickory. "Where's Squirrel?" he asked. "It ain't nighttime. Here we let him in the club and he never shows up no more."

"He had to go to Memphis with his folks again."

"What they do all the time in Memphis?"

"They got family there."

A pickup stopped in the drive, and Ike Montgomery got out. He stopped at the bottom step and stared at Jubal's knife.

"Where'd you get that knife, boy?" he asked.

"A man gave it to me," Jubal said. There wasn't a trace of fear in his voice, and he sat up taller.

Ike held out his hand. Jubal gave him the knife.

Ike looked at it closely, turning it over in his hand, then his eyes bored into Jubal. "You take this off his body?" he asked. His fist tightened around the knife.

"No, sir," Jubal said firmly. "He said he wanted me to have it."

Ike continued to stare at Jubal for what seemed like forever and a day, then he slowly held out his hand and gave the knife back. Jubal quickly shoved it into his pocket.

Poppa pushed open the back door. "I thought I heard somebody drive up," he said to Ike. "Come on in."

After they were inside, I said to Jubal, "Maybe he's going to tell him now about us being on his property and finding his father."

"Naw," said Jubal firmly. "He ain't gonna tell no-body nothing."

Ike left in a few minutes. He said nothing to us as he passed.

Jubal reminded me about the catfish Glory was cooking, and I stepped inside the house to tell Mama. I wouldn't be long, I said.

"You ain't going nowhere," Poppa said. "I'm sick and tired of you running around with those people. Your mama is fixing supper and you can eat right here with the rest of us."

I made a face at Poppa. "Jubal is right outside," I said softly.

"We're only having tuna fish sandwiches, Angus," Mama said. "I don't mind—"

"Don't contradict me in front of him, Dakota. If I say he ain't going, he ain't going. And I don't want to hear another word about it."

Jubal was gone when I went back outside. I wondered if he'd heard what Poppa said.

Later, after I went to bed, I lay in the darkness sweating. The oscillating fan on the chest of drawers slowly moved back and forth, but the air was thick and sticky. I thought about the angel Gabriel and Curtis Miller.

A dog from another farm barked. And I heard a screech owl crying. It sounded just like a baby. The grandfather clock in the front room chimed eleven times and, when I was beginning to drift off into sleep, twelve times.

TWENTY-SIX

UNCLE CHICAGO TOLD ME at breakfast the next morning that Curtis Miller was in the hospital in Tupelo. Reverend Graham and a deacon took him.

"I don't know if he is going to make it or not," he said glumly. "A gang of men rushed into his home and dragged him outside. He had a pistol in his hand, but they snatched it away from him. They surrounded him in the middle of the street and kicked him and beat him with a bullwhip. One of his eyes was torn out." He paused then said, "And it didn't have to happen. Why in the world didn't he get away?"

I really didn't care a whole lot what happened to Curtis Miller. What I was worried about was Ike Montgomery. "Jubal thinks Ike Montgomery was involved with Marcellus's death," I said.

"He's wrong."

"But—"

"I said he's wrong."

I wondered if the fact that Uncle Chicago and Ike

had been friends since childhood kept him from even considering the idea. He was like that. He wasn't friends with everybody, but it didn't matter whether you were of the white or Negro persuasion, if you were his friend he would die for you and refuse to think anything bad about you.

Later in the morning Jubal and I went by Squirrel's house. We were planning to work some on the Scorpions' Lair. We'd bought some brown and green paint and wanted to start painting. Nobody was home. We went on to the Lair and worked till lunchtime. Jubal had to go to work then.

That night I was watching television about eight-thirty when Squirrel knocked on the door and asked me to come outside.

"Where you been?" I asked. "We came by for you—"

"We've been in Memphis, and we're leaving now."

"For where?"

"I mean for good. We're leaving and never coming back."

"What are you talking about?"

"My mother is packing suitcases and my father is talking to Mr. Wrightson. He wants to sell the store and our house. Right now."

"Why?"

"My father says it won't be a cross burning next time, but our house. They hate Jews as much as coloreds, he said."

"But . . . where will you go?"

"Memphis. That's where our relatives are. My father's brothers insist we get out of here right now. Only I'm not supposed to tell anyone. So don't tell. Except Jubal, of course. It will be another Scorpion secret." He tried to smile. "I'll just have to be a member in absentia."

I just stood there. I didn't know what to say. It didn't make any sense.

He pressed his lips together and made a face. Then he said, "I don't want to go. I want to stay and fight. I can't stand the thought that Reno McCarthy and them will think they ran us off."

He stuck out his hand and I took it. "Promise me you'll get even for me. For the Scorpions," he said, squeezing my hand.

I squeezed back and said, "I promise."

I watched him in the dim light of the moon as he walked down to the road then across to his side. Then he faded into the darkness.

TWENTY-SEVEN

MR. KOGAN LEFT HIS DOGS with Uncle Chicago, since they couldn't have five beagles in their apartment in Memphis. Uncle Chicago told me he had no earthly idea what he was going to do with them, since he didn't hunt, and offered to pay me to feed them. I agreed, but three days later an old man up the highway who raised beagles made an offer for them. Uncle Chicago accepted and sent the money to Mr. Kogan.

I wrote and mailed another letter. This one was to Mr. Wrightson.

> We know you and your friends burned the cross in the Kogan's yard. We will not let this cowardly act go unavenged.
>
> The Scorpions

On Saturday morning, Uncle Chicago was very upset.

"What's wrong?" I asked as I took a bowl down from the cabinet over the sink.

"A friend of mine is missing," he said. And that was all he said.

After Alvina arrived, he set us right to painting the skull of a cow he'd found earlier that week in the woods. He kept walking outside onto the front porch. He would stand looking down the road for a while and then would come back in, pour himself more coffee, sit on the couch for a few minutes, then get up and go back onto the porch again.

Alvina hadn't spoken a word since she'd arrived. She was slapping paint onto a Masonite panel like she was attacking it, trying to hurt it. Her cow's skull was emerging as a chalky grotesque mask resembling a Klansman's hood.

She took her palette knife and mixed cadmium red light with a little alizarin crimson until it was the color of blood and with the knife slashed across the top of the skull.

"What in the world is wrong with you?" I asked.

She turned and glared at me. "Nothing, Chicken Coop. Nothing you would understand." She made another slash with the palette knife, digging deep through the painted skull to the very surface of the panel.

And that was it. She said nothing else.

Bessie arrived and stood on the porch with Uncle Chicago. We could hear them talking through the screen door.

"I've been by his house," he said. "His car's there but he's not. He hasn't been to work since Wednesday."

"I keep praying," said Bessie. "I just pray to the Lord that he is safe wherever he is." She placed her hand on his arm and added, "It's not your fault."

Uncle Chicago didn't reply.

"You need to go to the sheriff," she said.

"Sure," he answered.

Then she left.

A few minutes later, Alvina cleaned up and left.

"What's going on?" I asked.

Uncle Chicago sighed. "I can't talk about it. And I don't feel well. I'm going to lie down."

"Can I do anything for you?"

"No," he said, walking into the bedroom. He closed the door. I'd never seen him do that.

That afternoon Glory sent Jubal to take his grandmother a basket of fresh tomatoes from her garden. "Mind what you're doing now," she said.

I went with him.

Auntie Rachel was upset as soon as she saw the basket. "Take 'em back," she moaned. "I don't need no more trouble. Miss Sarah gonna be after me sure 'nough now. Take 'em back."

"But, Grandma, these came from Mama's garden."

"Don't fool with me now, boy. You make more trouble for me than any mother ought to expect." She rose from her rocker. "And how come you go and get Toby all mad? He be your cousin, boy, just as much as he be Ike's. Y'all got to get along."

"I'm Jubal, Grandma."

"Talk to him," she said to me. "Make him be good. Tell him to watch that fool mouth of his. Now, y'all get them tomatoes away from me."

"Miss Sarah been dead for a long time, Grandma. And Mr. Gideon be dead too. You know that."

She gave him a scornful glare, then shuffled into the house and slammed the door.

"Was she meaning Toby McCarthy?" I asked, remembering Reno's father and Ike were first cousins.

"Who knows what she ever means?" said Jubal.

As soon as we reached Jubal's place, I got on my scooter and rode to Uncle Chicago's. He was gessoing a canvas and listened as I repeated word for word what Auntie Rachel had said.

"I think she's confused," he said. "Or, did you ever stop to think it could be another Toby? I've known lots of Tobys in my life."

I hadn't. Toby McCarthy was the only one I'd ever heard of.

The next morning as we rode to church Bessie grumbled about the road, the dust, the heat, and that if she started sweating it was going to ruin her new dress. In Sunday school she never laughed once. The class began to get bored. She turned on us boys. "Why can't you all ever even read your lesson before you get here?" she said. "Why do I bother?" Then she walked out.

It was still fifteen minutes till time for the worship service. The adults were having class in the sanctuary, so we went outside and stood around talking till the bell rang.

I had never seen Bessie so agitated. I couldn't imagine what was wrong.

Reverend Graham preached on Job and how everything was taken away from him, how the messengers came and told him about one disaster after another, but God eventually saw him through.

"So it is with us," he said. "Sometimes we think we are in control and everything is going good. Then a messenger comes with bad news. But God will see us through." There was something so strange about his voice that people in the congregation were unusually silent.

"And so I bring very, very bad news for you and for me and for all God's people," he said. He paused and his lips trembled. "Gabriel is gone."

There were confused looks on everyone's faces. It was as if each of us was trying to understand what he meant. How "gone"?

The minister continued. "He was willing to help us. But he can't do that no more. I don't have to tell you what that means." He finished his sermon with a very subdued and abbreviated praise-song.

People filed out of the sanctuary afterward, looking

hopelessly at each other, and stood around in small groups. Mothers gathered their children to themselves and held them.

Bessie had tears in her eyes as she drove me home. "Pray for Gabriel," she said as she let me out. "Maybe he's not dead. Maybe he will be able to come back."

TWENTY-EIGHT

WHEN I ARRIVED Monday morning, Uncle Chicago
was still in his pajamas. He didn't even look at the
paper but sat at the table sipping his coffee.

I pulled the paper over to my side of the table and
began to read the articles out loud to him. There had
been a firebombing at the civil rights headquarters in
Canton, Mississippi.

"What's a Molotov cocktail?" I asked.

"I can't even think right now," he said.

"Sir?"

"I'm sorry. I just don't feel well."

"What's wrong?"

He just shook his head and went into his bedroom
and closed the door. I knew he was either sick or very
upset.

I went home and washed my scooter. I debated
in my mind about telling Nana or Mama that Uncle
Chicago wasn't well. I decided not to. I thought he
wouldn't like that unless he said it was okay.

After lunch I went fishing at the pond. I kept thinking about this Gabriel thing all day. All I knew for sure—although no one had confirmed this for me—was that someone knew about the meetings at Wrightson's store and what the Klansmen were going to do before they did it. I wasn't exactly sure how many warnings had been passed on to Reverend Graham. Some he had announced in church. Probably some he had given in private. And whoever was giving him the information was now gone.

I also knew that none of those men meeting at Mr. Wrightson's could afford being seen going to see the pastor. Somehow, the information had to go to someone else who, in turn, told the preacher. But which man? I had no idea, except, of course, I knew it wasn't Poppa. And it couldn't be Reno. Or Mr. Wrightson.

I tried to picture the others I'd seen there—Coach Turner, Brother Simmons and his son Bobby Mac, Tom Jackson and his father, Moses Jackson, Guin Peoney, Casey Donald, and, of course, Ike Montgomery.

And I thought about Ike letting us take the lumber, and how Mr. Gideon wanted us to take him to Aunt Rachel's, and how Mr. Gideon gave Jubal that pocket-knife. That was strange. And talk about strange, what about all the times Auntie Rachel thought we were people who were already grown-up?

And what did she mean about them being cousins?

Who was whose cousin? I think she meant Marcellus and Toby. But how . . . ?

And I thought about Ike Montgomery that night coming back from seeing Uncle Chicago, and Uncle Chicago saying he'd come to give him a friendly warning.

Warning?

Of course! It suddenly all made sense.

I snatched my line out of the water and threw the pole down on the bank and ran back up to the house. My scooter was parked in the shed.

I raced over to Uncle Chicago's, slid to a stop in the dirt in front of his house, bounded up the steps and into the front room.

Uncle Chicago was sitting in a chair at the table, thumbing through an old sketchbook. He looked up at me.

"It's Ike Montgomery, ain't it?" I blurted out. "Gabriel is Ike Montgomery!"

He laid aside the sketchbook and said softly, "Yes."

I walked to the table and sat down.

Uncle Chicago buried his face in his hands. "I asked him to do it," he said. "I made him feel he owed it."

"Because of Marcellus."

"Yes, because of Marcellus."

"He was more than just a friend, wasn't he?"

He nodded his head in his hands.

"Gideon Montgomery was Marcellus's father, just

like he was Ike's, wasn't he? That's how come Marcellus was Toby's cousin."

"Yes," he said very softly.

I felt my face flush. Uncle Chicago had lied to me.

He sensed my mind. "Now, listen," he said. "I didn't actually lie. What I *said* was, 'I think she is confused.' Well? Wasn't she?"

I didn't respond.

"And I said there were lots of people named Toby."

"But—"

"Okay. I misled you. I was afraid for you to know too much. These are horrible times. And I was also trying to protect . . ." He paused, then said, "I was trying to protect Ike's identity. I told Bessie the information came to me through Gabriel's wife. I told Reverend Graham the same thing. And the FBI man in Tupelo. And that's all I would tell them. I never mentioned Ike's name. And, you know, Ike wasn't married. I thought if anybody slipped up, they would think whoever it was was married and nobody would figure out it was him." He looked at me. "He was also trying to find out who killed Marcellus. He knew he didn't hang himself and he told me a couple of weeks ago that he was very close to getting the proof that Toby and a couple of others did it."

"What did they do with him?"

"Only God and the Klan know."

"Did you talk to the sheriff?" I asked, remembering what Bessie suggested.

"I did yesterday afternoon. He said he'd look into it."

"What's going to happen now?"

He shook his head slowly. "There's no one else who would let us know what they're up to so we can warn the church. Think about those guys who are meeting there at Wrightson's store. Including my own brother-in-law. There's not a one of them who would do this."

And I knew he was right.

TWENTY-NINE

TUESDAY AFTERNOON Nana told me she had been in
the Ben Franklin to pick up some fabric when Johnny
Harris and two young women—one white and the
other colored—sat down at the lunch counter to be
served. The waitress completely ignored them. The
white woman kept demanding they be given a menu.
The waitress went on serving other customers and
never answered her a word.

"A lot of people were watching," she said. "After
about fifteen minutes they left. I'd never seen the colored girl or the white one. Someone said they are part
of that group that's come down from the North to stir
up trouble. I guess new law or not, they aren't going
to serve coloreds at the Ben Franklin."

"I know them," I said. "They're from California.
Tamara Feinstein and Esther Garrison. They're not
trying to stir up trouble. They're trying to help Negroes
register to vote."

Nana looked startled. I guess my voice was pretty loud.

"Cooper!" said Mama, who was sitting and reading a magazine. "Apologize to your grandmother for using that tone of voice."

I sighed. "Okay. I'm sorry." Then I went to my room.

I stretched out on my bed. What was going to happen now? I knew there was no way, once Mr. Wrightson and the others heard about the incident at the Ben Franklin, they wouldn't do something.

Curtis Miller had only been home from the hospital a week and was still in bed. The others who'd been warned had run off and no one was saying where they were. But, like Reverend Graham said, Gabriel was gone now.

When Poppa came in from work he walked into my room. He was still wearing his work clothes with pig grease and blood all over him. "There's an important meeting at Wrightson's tonight," he said. "Don't go running off after supper and pretending you don't hear me when I call. You understand?"

I didn't respond.

"I said, *do you understand?*" I could hear his teeth grinding.

"Yes, sir," I mumbled. I wanted to ask him about Ike Montgomery but I knew if I did it would endanger Uncle Chicago.

He went to take his bath. Supper would be in about an hour. Glory was already in the kitchen. Jubal hadn't come over to work out and Alvina didn't come either.

The Klan was going to get Johnny. I knew it.

I walked out onto the front porch. I blinked my eyes a couple of times, looking at the sky. The sun was still intense, glaring. And I knew what I had to do.

I rode my scooter to Uncle Chicago's. Bessie's car was parked in front. I yanked open the screen door and went inside.

He was sitting on the couch talking with Bessie.

"I need to talk to you," I said firmly, looking at him. "Alone, if you don't mind."

Bessie gave Uncle Chicago a raised-eyebrow look. He shrugged in response. Bessie smiled and said it was time for her to go anyway.

Once she was gone, Uncle Chicago turned to me. "Well?"

"I could be Gabriel," I said.

"What?" I think he was too shocked to laugh.

"I could be Gabriel. Poppa says there's a meeting at Wrightson's tonight and he wants me to go. I *have* to go, he says. I could tell you what they were planning, just like Ike did, and you could tell Bessie."

He smiled. "So, you figured that out, eh?"

"You and Bessie talk all the time. You've been painting together for years. Everybody thinks the two of you are half nuts anyway. You tell her, and she tells Reverend Graham. That's how it works, isn't it?"

His smile faded. "I love you too much, Sport. It's too dangerous. They've killed Ike and probably loaded his body down with chains and dumped him in a river or swamp somewhere."

"I know it's dangerous. But I can't let them do what they are going to do."

"What are they going to do?"

I told him about the incident at Ben Franklin. "I can be Gabriel," I repeated.

"No. And that's final. No discussion."

I went to the front door, turned back to him and said, "You can't stop me." Then I left.

THIRTY

COACH TURNER GRINNED at me as soon as I came into the back room at Wrightson's grocery store with Poppa. "This is one of my boys," he said with pride. "I want you all to be looking for him this fall. I think this boy has got what it takes to play a lot of ball."

"Most of you have heard about what happened at the Ben Franklin today," said Mr. Wrightson as soon as everyone was seated. "It was one of our local boys, Johnny Harris, and two of those COFO workers. They're from California. We need to decide what, if anything, we're going to do about it."

"The problem with messing with these COFO people is that you get the FBI down on you so quick," said Coach Turner. "But we can deal with our own Negroes."

"They got the Freedom School out at the colored church," said Casey Donald. "That church is a hotbed of trouble."

"Johnny Harris is the brother of Jubal Harris," said

Reno McCarthy, looking at me. "I think they need to be taken care of like their daddy was."

"That's enough," his father said to him.

"I know Johnny Harris," Poppa said. "His mother works for us. I'll talk to her."

Mr. Wrightson gave Poppa a thoughtful look. "You do that," he said. "But this ain't over yet. We're still thinking about what we need to do."

"What are we going to do if they try to register to vote and bring the FBI with them?" Casey Donald asked.

"I've got my ax handle on the backseat of my car," said Moses Jackson. "If I so much as see one of them near the courthouse—"

"Just a minute," said Mr. Wrightson. "We don't need anybody going off on their own and doing anything. This is war, and you are soldiers for freedom, and you won't act without orders. Is that understood?"

Jackson gave a reluctant nod.

Wrightson looked around at the others. Each man nodded he understood.

"I want you to be ready," Wrightson said. "They probably think we're going to do something tonight, but that's where we keep them off guard. We did have a problem with information getting out and into the wrong hands, but that's been taken care of. But on this . . . well, I'll let you know."

"But don't wait too long," said Jackson.

Mr. Wrightson smiled. "We've got some very big

ideas, and I think you all will be pleased," he said. "Very pleased. And it won't be all that long."

His smile faded, and he asked, "Does anyone know anything about a group called the Scorpions?"

I kept my eyes on him and didn't blink, but I stopped breathing.

Reno spoke up, "Yeah," he said. "And we need to get them, too."

"Who are they?"

"I don't know. I just heard of them."

Mr. Wrightson nodded. "Never mind," he said, smiling again. "But I will find out who they are. I always do."

We left then.

Going home, I asked Poppa, "What did Reno mean about Johnny and Jubal being taken care of like Marcellus was?"

Poppa gave a derisive snort. "He's an idiot," he said. "He don't know what he's talking about."

I stared out the side window into the darkness. I wasn't too sure about that. Not at all.

On Thursday afternoon, Glory, Jubal, and Alvina all came to the house together. Glory winked at me and said, "Turnip greens tonight, Cooper. Look at you smile. I thought you'd like that."

She went on into the kitchen and Jubal and Alvina were standing at the back steps with me. I hadn't seen Jubal in a couple of days.

I pulled him aside. "Listen," I said to him. "Reno McCarthy is nuts. He's determined to beat me up, but I think he wants to *kill* you."

Jubal threw out his chest. "Let him come on," he said. "I ain't running no more." He sounded just like Johnny.

"But, this is serious and—"

"When the rest of them jump in Saturday, I'll be jumping in too," he said. "You can tell that to Reno McCarthy."

"Shut up, fool," said Alvina, coming toward him.

"Jumping in what?" I asked.

"You all's swimming pool at Warren Park, that's what," Jubal said.

"I told you to shut up," said Alvina. "You want him to tell Mr. Angus?"

"Jump in all you want, Fly," I said to her. "I don't care what you do."

The back screen door opened and Glory said, "Get in here girl, and help me. What you getting all riled up about, anyways?"

"Nothing," she said, giving me a threatening look. "Nothing at all."

THIRTY-ONE

ON FRIDAY AFTERNOON, I had just finished washing my hands after changing the oil in the scooter when Mama came home all upset.

"What is going on around here?" she said as I helped her bring in the groceries from the car.

"What? What?" I asked.

"I went by Blue Star to get some pork chops for Sunday—you know I like theirs so much better than Wrightson's—and so I was passing Warren Park. I saw all these cars and people standing around the swimming pool, so I pulled over to get a better look. I thought somebody had drowned. And I saw several dump trucks and they had taken down the chain-link fence around the pool, and I saw this man walking back from over there—I think it was Ruth Clare Adams's husband but I haven't seen them in so long I couldn't be sure. Anyway, I asked him what was going on and he said the city was filling in the swimming pool in case any coloreds should try to stage a swim-in. Can you imagine? Filling in the pool? I'm telling you I just don't know what's going to happen when school starts back. If it does."

A few minutes later, Glory arrived with Alvina and Jubal. "I wants you to get right on peeling them potatoes," Glory said to Alvina as she walked up the steps.

"I'll be in in a minute," Alvina replied.

"Not in a minute. Come on now," she said, going into the kitchen.

Both Jubal and Alvina were looking at me as if waiting for me to speak. "I heard," I said.

"Johnny says this didn't just happen," Alvina said. There was acid in her tone. "They knew we was coming tomorrow and that's why they did it."

Jubal was looking at me but he didn't say anything.

"Well, I didn't tell anybody," I said, knowing that's what both of them were thinking.

"Yeah, sure," she said. "Just like you ain't ever been to one of them meetings at Wrightson's store, either." She glared at me as she walked up the steps and into the kitchen.

After we were sitting down for supper, Poppa told me that we had to go out later. Mama and Nana exchanged looks but didn't say anything. Then Mama told them about seeing the city pool being filled in.

"That's the most foolish thing I ever heard of," Nana said, passing me the corn bread. "Why would any coloreds want to go to our pool? They have one of their own."

Nobody answered. If there was a pool for coloreds, I certainly had never heard of it. The only two places I knew Jubal ever swam were in our pond and in the big bend at Bear Creek.

The meeting at Wrightson's was at eight o'clock.

"Okay, tell 'em," Mr. Wrightson said once everyone was together and seated and quiet.

Casey Donald wiped his mouth with the back of his hand and said, "Marie told me she was at Blackie's filling station this afternoon and got out the car while the boy was filling the tank to get a pack of cigarettes, and when she walked inside, there was these two colored boys standing off to the side and one of them looked at her funny."

"What do you mean?" asked Coach Turner. "How funny?"

"You know," said Casey. "Like he was smiling and just scaring her and he knew he was doing it, Marie said."

Everyone was silent for a moment, then Mr. Wrightson said, "Did she know who this colored boy was?"

"Yeah. She said it was the same one she'd seen at Ben Franklin the other day. She was there and saw him with that Yankee white girl and colored girl from California sitting at the lunch counter. She swears it was the very same one."

Mr. Wrightson nodded gravely. "Johnny Harris."

He looked at Poppa. "Angus, you were going to talk to his mother."

Poppa cleared his throat and said, "I did. She said she'd speak to him."

"Didn't seem to do any good," said Moses Jackson.

"We've got something really big in the works," Wrightson said. "I'll let you all know about that when it's time. But first, we need to take care of this business." He paused, looked around at everyone, then said, "We'll meet back here at eleven o'clock. It should be quiet and dark in the quarters by then. And I know which house the Harrises live in."

THIRTY-TWO

RIGHT AFTER WE GOT HOME, I rode over to Uncle Chicago's. It was a clear night and the moon was almost full.

"They're going to get Johnny Harris tonight," I told him. "They're meeting back at Wrightson's store at eleven o'clock."

Uncle Chicago, who was already in his pajamas, began changing immediately. "Okay," he said. "I'll take care of it. Go home now."

I did. Poppa saw me coming back into the house. He was in the front room with Nana and Mama watching the Alfred Hitchcock show on television.

"Where've you been?" he asked.

"On my scooter," I said. "I changed the oil today." That was all I said. There certainly wasn't any lie in that. He didn't ask anything else.

Shortly after ten, I went to my room, undressed, turned out the light, and got in bed. Moonlight flowed softly through the open window and fell onto the floor near the chest of drawers. The sounds of the night were peaceful—the murmuring of insects and an occasional dog bark. The quiet before the storm, as Bessie sometimes said.

And I wondered if Bessie had already come and gone to the quarters to see Reverend Graham. Surely she had. It had been almost an hour since I told Uncle Chicago. Johnny Harris should be on a highway leaving town by now.

Who would be driving him and to where? They could be at the bus station in Tupelo in less than an hour. There were buses coming all through the night. What would Mr. Wrightson and the others do once they got to the Harris's and found out he was gone?

Thoughts and questions kept bouncing around in my mind. I didn't know whether Poppa was going or not. I knew within the hour I might be hearing gunshots from the quarters. By then, though, Johnny Harris could even be on a Greyhound headed for Memphis.

My door opened and the overhead light came on. "Get up," Poppa said. "Put your clothes on."

I didn't move. My eyes sprang open in surprise only for a moment when the light came on, but then I shut them tight.

"Hurry up," he said, coming to the bed and shaking

my shoulder. "We need to be out of here in five minutes."

Most everyone was already at Wrightson's when we arrived, and almost everyone except Poppa and me had a shotgun or a rifle. Poppa did have his pistol stuck down in his belt. My heart was pounding. I wanted to run, to get away. This couldn't be happening.

"You won't have to get out the car," Poppa told me as we all gathered into three cars. "But I think it's important that you be here."

Four of us rode with Moses Jackson. Beside him and his son, Tom, there was me and Poppa and Casey Donald. The mood in the car was like at deer camp. An almost giddy excitement.

I was sitting in the backseat between Casey and Poppa. Casey had his twelve-gauge automatic shotgun between his legs. "I told Marie that boy would be sorry he ever laid eyes on her," he said. "That other boy just got one eye knocked out. I want to see both of Johnny Harris's eyes on the ground."

I was breathing very shallow. What if someone had followed me to Chicago's? What if someone had followed him? What if something happened and the message didn't get through? What if Jubal and Alvina and Jerome and Glory and Johnny were still in their house, still in bed sleeping peaceful-like and not even knowing what was coming?

We were the last of the three cars. I could see the taillights of the two cars ahead. The lead car slowed down at the turnoff road to the quarters, then turned, followed by the second car and us.

There were no streetlights in the quarters, but by the light of the moon you could see each house clearly. We were getting close to Jubal's house. Casey Donald pulled a white hood over his head.

The cars stopped right in front of the house. Mr. Jackson and Tom and Casey threw open their doors and jumped out. When the doors opened, the dome light came on and I instinctively ducked, fleeing the light just like a rat, and covered my head with my hands.

The doors slammed shut and the car was dark again. I sat up. Torches were lit and several men were already on Jubal's porch. Some were masked, some weren't. One kicked the door open and men with guns and torches charged into the house.

I could see the torchlight and the men through the windows as they moved from room to room. In a couple of minutes they came onto the front porch, then stepped down onto the ground. Someone fired a shotgun in the air. More shots followed.

"Johnny Harris!" yelled one. I think it was Casey Donald. "Come out here!"

There was not a light on in any house around. All was perfectly still. Even the dog that lived across the street was silent or gone.

"There's nobody home!" said Poppa. "They ain't here!"

Was I imagining it? Or did his voice sound as relieved as I suddenly felt. *Thank you God! Thank you that they aren't home! Yes, thank you, thank you, thank you!*

The men went back into the house with the torches. Immediately, the curtains in the windows went up in flames. Then the men came and stood on the porch, looking back into the house. I could hear the cracking, popping, and sizzling as the flames spread quickly inside the house.

The men ran to the cars. I ducked my head this time before the dome light came on.

The cars started, headlights flashed on, and we raced out of the quarters. I looked back over my shoulder, out the rearview window. Flames were shooting out the windows and the front door.

"They knew it!" said Moses Jackson, spitting out the words. "They knew we was coming!"

"But how? How?" demanded Casey.

Jackson gave a cynical laugh as he turned onto the highway to town. "Somebody *told* them. Somebody who was at that meeting not two hours ago at Wrightson's told them." Nobody else said anything the rest of the way to town.

After we got in our pickup and started home, Poppa said, "I was just as glad they weren't there, to tell you the truth."

I nodded. Me too. A thousand times *me too.*

THIRTY-THREE

IF I SLEPT AT ALL that night it could only have been for a few hours. Waking or sleeping, roaring flames chased me, sucked at me, tormented me. I thought I was being choked by smoke, and the image from the rear window as we were leaving the quarters of Jubal's house exploding in fire was never out of my mind.

The next morning, after finishing my route, I went to Chicago's. There was a note taped to the front door. "Gone to the quarters. There is cereal on the table and milk in the icebox if you want breakfast. Come over when you can."

I wasn't at all hungry. I desperately wanted to go to the quarters myself to see that everyone was all right, that they were safe and sound, but, at the same time, I felt ashamed and guilty at having been there. Wasn't the one who sat in the car and waited while the bank robbers were inside the bank just as guilty? Wasn't that what being an accomplice was all about?

But I knew I had to go.

When I arrived at the quarters, a crowd was standing around the smoldering rubble where the house had been. Only the chimney and the foundation brick pillars remained standing. The blackened wringer washer Glory was so proud of lay on its side in the area where the front porch had been. No fire truck had come. Luckily, there'd been no wind and neither of the houses beside it caught fire.

I saw Alvina and Jubal. Her eyes were puffy like she'd been crying. His face was hard, and he stood to the side with his hands on his hips, staring with unblinking eyes into the smoke still rising from the ashes.

Uncle Chicago, Bessie, and Reverend Graham were talking with two white men in dark suits and ties and hats.

"FBI," Auntie Deliah said to me. She had a snuff stick in her mouth and was making clucking sounds. I walked over and stood beside Uncle Chicago. I heard him call one of the men "Mr. Shapiro."

I tugged at Uncle Chicago's sleeve. "I need to talk to you," I said.

"Just a minute," he said, turning back to the agent.

"We have to have people willing to come forward and testify," Mr. Shapiro said.

Sheriff Skinner and a deputy arrived, walked around a bit, looking at the remains of the house, then came back to where the FBI men were standing.

"Faulty wiring?" suggested the sheriff.

Mr. Shapiro, who had been jotting in a notebook,

snapped it closed and said, "We have some names, Sheriff. There are witnesses who saw the men who did this."

"They saw in the dark?" Sheriff Skinner asked with a smile.

"The men were carrying torches. And we have one witness who was looking out when the cars stopped. We'll be questioning more people."

Jerome Suddith was poking through some ashes with a pole. "Lord have mercy," he said, his voice breaking.

I walked over to see.

It was the charred remains of his big Bible. He tried to rake the book towards him across the hot and smoking ashes, but it crumbled apart.

Glory moved beside him and put her arms around him. "But we all be safe," she said. "Even our Johnny." She lifted up her head, looked to the sky, and raised one hand. "Thank you, precious Jesus. Thank you for sending the angel Gabriel back to us. Thank you, thank you, thank you."

Uncle Chicago motioned me to follow him away from everyone else. "What's wrong?" he asked. "You look awful."

"I was here last night," I said. "Poppa made me come. But I stayed in the car. So did Poppa. I don't think anyone saw me."

"It's okay," he said, placing his hand on my shoulder.

"And they know somebody warned Johnny Harris. They know it."

"I'm sure they do." He studied my face. "You don't have to do this anymore. You know that."

I swallowed. "But . . . Mr. Wrightson said they are planning something really big."

"Oh?"

"But he didn't say what it is."

"I'm not going to ask you to go to any more meetings. You do whatever you feel comfortable with."

"Okay," I said, looking at Sheriff Skinner. "Did the sheriff find out anything?"

He made a contemptuous sound. "He told me that Russell Wrightson said Ike was in his store the other day and told him he was going to California to visit a cousin of his for a few weeks."

"Mr. Harrington," Agent Shapiro called out to Uncle Chicago. "Can I see you for a moment?"

Ronald Ritter was taking pictures of everyone. Sheriff Skinner kept scowling in his direction.

I walked over to Jubal. "I'm sorry," I said. "Where did you all go?"

"Go?"

"So you weren't in the house."

He nodded toward the houses across the street. "Over there," he said. "As soon as Reverend Graham come, we got out. And Johnny left. He didn't even pack."

Alvina turned her head slightly as she looked at me. "Was Mr. Angus with them?"

"W-what?"

"I don't stutter. You heard me."

Before I could answer, Esther Garrison stepped up to us and gave both Jubal and Alvina a hug. "I'm so glad y'all got out," she said.

She looked at me and smiled. Her teeth were perfectly white and perfectly even. "Cooper, I had a friend once whose name was George," she said. "He helped me out when we were young. Just about your age." She looked from me to Alvina. "And here Cooper has already helped me out. I know a good man when I see one."

She grinned at me again.

And behind me, I heard a man say to someone, "Well, there was three cars. That's what Cheeter said. He was looking out his window. And he said when they opened their door the car lights inside came on and he saw them. He said he recognized some of them."

I felt like I could hardly breathe.

THIRTY-FOUR

AFTER LUNCH Nana gave me a letter to mail to her sister in Memphis. "I forgot to get this out to the road before the postman passed," she said.

The post office was on Simpson Street, a half block west of the courthouse. I parked my scooter at the curb.

Mr. Mushlin, a bald-headed man who was shorter than me, was the postmaster. He was putting up mail when I walked in. He glanced at me.

"Already got a stamp," I said, holding up the letter.

"Just drop it in," he said, sliding a letter into a box.

On the counter were two wire baskets, one marked "Local" and the other "Out-of-Town." I laid Nana's letter in the out-of-town basket and returned to the door.

Ronald Ritter was stepping inside. It was the first time I'd seen him without his camera. He looked at me and gave a start. "Oh," he said. "You."

"Hey," I replied.

He was holding a manila envelope in one hand and quickly drew it back. Then he smiled. "So. Mailing a letter?" he asked.

"Yeah." My eyes were on his envelope.

"Something for my mother," he said. "A . . . a gift." He passed by me toward the counter, and I went outside.

Ritter's car was parked in front of my scooter. I started the scooter, turned around in the middle of the street, and headed toward home.

Why was he so nervous? He looked almost scared.

I had just passed the square. I braked by the hardware store, pulled into the alley, and parked. Hadn't Uncle Chicago said to watch out for Ronald Ritter? What did he suspect?

And then it hit me. What if . . . ?

I left the scooter and walked back toward the post office. I paused in front of the florist shop at the corner and looked up the street. Ritter was getting into his car. I watched him pull away from the curb. As soon as he was out of sight, I sprinted back to the post office and rushed inside.

Mr. Mushlin looked up.

"I . . . I think I forgot to put a stamp on my letter," I said, stepping to the letter baskets.

Mr. Mushlin frowned as he waited for me to check.

The manila envelope was right on top in the out-of-town basket. I picked it up and, as I held it to one side, read the address. The envelope was bulky, thick.

I lifted Nana's letter for Mr. Mushlin to see. "No, it does have a stamp," I said.

Mr. Mushlin looked back at the stack of mail in his hand.

Outside the post office, I closed my eyes and, just like in recall drawing, pictured the address on the envelope. It wasn't anything or anyone I was familiar with. But it certainly, as far as I could tell, wasn't addressed to Ritter's mother.

As soon as I got to Uncle Chicago's house, I rushed inside, snatched up a pencil and a piece of paper, and wrote the address down exactly as I remembered it.

"What in the world . . . ?" said Uncle Chicago.

I told him about seeing Ritter, how nervous he acted, and showed him the address. The recipient was "M.S.S.C" with a post office box in Jackson.

Uncle Chicago stared at the initials for a moment, then went to the telephone and dialed a number. "Hello, Tom? This is James Harrington." He told Tom the initials and the address. "Is this what I think it is?" he asked.

He listened and kept his eyes on me. Then he smiled and winked at me. "Okay," he said. "Keep the faith, brother." He replaced the receiver.

"You did great," he said to me. "Ritter mailed the envelope to the Mississippi State Sovereignty Commission."

I knew about the Sovereignty Commission. Uncle

Chicago said that it was a spy-type agency under the governor.

"And I think I know what he sent them," he said.

"Rolls of film?" I asked.

He nodded again. "I need to see Reverend Graham right away."

In the morning, I snapped on my tie and went onto the porch to wait for Bessie. Mama was sitting in the swing, smoking a cigarette.

"Your daddy said he didn't think you ought to be going to Bessie's church anymore," she said. Poppa was still asleep.

Bessie's car arrived. "He didn't tell me that," I said, walking down the steps.

"He will," she called after me.

As we drove away, Bessie said, "Reverend Graham and the deacons went to Ronald Ritter last night and told him he'd better make himself scarce and never be seen around here again."

I didn't respond. Uncle Chicago said it would be best if no one knew I was the one who'd found him out.

"He was the one," she continued. "He was telling the Sovereignty Commission everything we were going to do beforehand, and the Sovereignty Commission made sure Russell Wrightson got the information."

I looked out the windows at the trees whipping past.

"Everything okay?" she asked.

"Fine," I said.

We rode the rest of the way in silence.

Bessie slowed to a crawl as we drove over the plank bridge just before the church. Several men from the church were standing around the bridge. They waved and we waved in return. Two of them had crowbars in their hands.

At church everyone was still talking about the fire. No one asked where Johnny Harris had gone. The only thing that mattered was that he was safely away. Several people said how glad they were that Gabriel had come back.

After Sunday school I walked over to Alvina. I didn't think she would apologize for having implied I'd been informing the Klan, but I did think she might acknowledge that she knew I wasn't the one. She gave me a distasteful look and walked away.

I caught up with Jubal, and we sat together in the worship service. In his sermon, Reverend Graham told us that Negroes in Jackson were boycotting the stores again after twenty-three folks had been refused service. He said that we all might be called upon to do the same thing in Chulosa if changes didn't come about quick.

After church, as I was walking out the front door, I saw cloth flour sacks on the floor against the back wall. I asked Bessie about it.

"Just getting a project ready," she said with a wink.

"What kind of project?"

"I promised not to say anything to anybody yet," she said.

I wondered if she'd promised not to tell *anybody* or just me.

The following Wednesday morning, I scanned the *Journal* as I rolled up my eighty-three papers and stuffed them into the canvas route bag. The main headline all the way across the top of the front page was about navy planes blasting PT boat bases in some place called North Vietnam.

Below the fold of the front page, near the bottom, was a small article about FBI agents in Philadelphia, Mississippi, finding three bodies at a dam site that authorities strongly suspected were the three COFO workers who'd been missing since June 21. The bodies would be flown by helicopters to the University of Mississippi Medical Center in Jackson for identification. They were working from dental records and fingerprints.

I hurried through my route.

"I know, I know," Uncle Chicago said when I brought him his paper. "Bessie came over last night. A friend from Meridian had phoned and told her."

He said he worried that the reaction throughout the state would be anger that somebody had to have helped the FBI, because they wouldn't have known to pick out that particular dam out of the hundreds around there unless somebody on the inside told them.

"What I'm afraid of is that these local pointed heads will think they need to do something to assert themselves," he said. "And that may be the 'big' thing Wrightson mentioned."

"I'm just waiting for them to call us to a meeting," I said.

He didn't reply.

I didn't have to wait long. Poppa told me at supper that Casey Donald had told him at the plant that afternoon that there was going to be a meeting at Wrightson's.

"What I've heard," said Brother Bill Simmons, the Methodist preacher, as soon as we were all together in the storeroom, "is that the informer was paid twenty-five thousand dollars."

"Then it was one of their own?" asked Coach Turner.

"Happens," said Mr. Wrightson. "Even in the best circles." He gave a wry smile and looked around the room.

"There's something that really bothers me," said Moses Jackson, holding a package of Red Man chewing tobacco in his hand and kneading a wad of tobacco. "Now I know he's your brother-in-law, Angus, but Chicago Harrington has been fooling around with col-oreds for years. He runs around with that crazy old colored woman, Bessie Summers, and no telling what they're putting people up to in the quarters. And she rides up in the front seat with him. That ought to tell you something." He spit into a Dixie cup. "I guess my point is, maybe we ought to teach him a lesson. Maybe just burn a cross in his front yard or something."

Poppa stiffened. "Bessie Summers is just a harmless old woman," he said. "And they're both artists. I doubt they know the first thing that is happening in the world around them."

"Chicago Harrington is not our problem," said Mr. Wrightson.

Everybody became very still and quiet.

He continued. "Johnny Harris and his family knew we were coming. I had told absolutely no one—*no one*—until we were all together at eight o'clock. We left here at nine and met again two hours later. In those two hours, someone in this room got word to Johnny Harris that we were coming." He paused and turned around slowly, looking into the eyes of each of us. When he looked at me, I almost wet my pants, but I didn't blink.

"I will tell you this," he said. "I *will* find out. I did before and I will again. And you will be made to suffer." He jabbed his finger toward each of us in turn. "And I mean *suffer.*"

There was a long silence. Then Mr. Wrightson said, "That's all for now. Meeting's adjourned."

THIRTY-FIVE

BEFORE THE WEEK WAS OUT, the FBI had questioned several men about the fire, including Mr. Wrightson, but they didn't come to our house, and they didn't arrest anybody. "Besides," Poppa told me, "they ain't got no one who's gonna come forward and say anything. Wrightson has put the word out that it wouldn't be good if any colored was seen talking to these federal people."

He said the FBI ought to be working up in New Jersey where, earlier in the week, two Negroes and three policemen were hurt in a race riot. "We can take care of our own problems," Poppa said.

Sunday morning I overheard Nana telling Poppa maybe it was time for me to start going to First Baptist. "He don't have to go nowhere," Poppa said. "None of us ever went to church and it didn't hurt us none."

I went outside to wait for Bessie in the swing. In my lap I had the bowl of Jell-O salad Mama had made. There were a lot of things I liked about my church, but one of the best things was our dinners-on-the-grounds. One was to be held that very morning, and I was excited about it. If I couldn't go to Oak Grove, I wasn't going anyplace, and that was that.

Bessie arrived and off we went. She had a basket of her homemade rolls covered with a red towel on the seat between us.

As we approached the plank bridge just before the church, Bessie slowed up and eased over the bridge. The boards groaned as I'd never heard them do before. And except for last Sunday, when the men were standing around the bridge, I had never known her to do anything but race over it before sliding to a stop at the church parking lot.

She noticed my perplexed look. "Old bridge," she explained. "Not as strong as it used to be."

In his prayer that morning, Reverend Graham not only prayed for the four girls killed in Birmingham, but for the families of Michael Schwerner, James Chaney, and Andrew Goodman. They were the three COFO workers found buried in the dam. He also prayed for Reverend Boyd from Memphis, who would be preaching the revival starting that very night.

In his sermon, Reverend Graham said we all had to live with the fact that right now the men who had done terrible things to us might go unpunished. He was looking at Jubal and Alvina as he said this.

"For now!" he said. "But a day is coming when God himself will bring his own vengeance. But that's for God to do. Not you and me. 'Vengeance is mine; I will repay, saith the Lord.'" He paused and slowly wiped his face with a large white handkerchief.

"And we got to forgive no matter how hard it hurts," he continued. "We cannot repay evil for evil. Never!"

I wondered what Jubal was thinking.

After the service, the women spread tablecloths over tables constructed of rough planks nailed between the oak trees on the north side of the church. The trees offered a heavy, cool shade from the wretchedness of the August sun.

Then they set out the food—platters of fried chicken and roast beef and ham and barbecued pork, bowls of butter beans and black-eyed peas and snap beans, and pork and beans with molasses and hamburger cooked in it, and cheese grits and casseroles, turnip greens and ears of corn, creamed corn, and half a dozen bowls of potato salad and several plates of deviled eggs, corn bread and muffins and rolls and biscuits, and cakes and pies and cobblers and a dozen different kinds of cookies.

While the women worked, a few men set up the gallon jugs of iced tea and shooed flies away from the tables. Most of the men, however, stood in the shade, smoking cigarettes and talking about the need for rain, the heat, their crops, and what President Johnson might do now that the bodies had been found.

I walked over to Jubal, who was standing with a

group of boys not far from the men. I had sat by him in Sunday school and church but he wouldn't talk. He had not said more than a word or two to me and then always in response to a direct question.

The boys were talking about football. Most of them, like Jubal, were planning to play at Washington once school started. Their practices were to begin in less than two weeks. I mentioned that I was going to start this year at guard at my school. No one even looked at me after I said that or acknowledged me in any way. Something seemed very wrong, but I had no idea what it was.

Shortly before it was time to eat, Reverend Graham and Bessie came out of the church. They were talking, and Bessie looked like she was about to cry. I couldn't imagine what they were talking about that was upsetting her so much.

Reverend Graham got everyone's attention and said the blessing. Then we all lined up to eat. I took a paper plate and piled it high with all my favorite things and, carrying the plate in one hand and a cup of tea in the other, walked toward the grassy hillside under the trees behind the church, where the boys were eating.

The girls were all sitting around the back steps of the church and giggling and talking. As I approached they fell silent, and as soon as I passed they began whispering.

I was no longer interested in the mound of food on my plate. In fact, there was a trembling in my stomach, and I didn't think I could eat a single bite, not even of fried chicken.

The boys also grew quiet as I approached. I stopped and didn't know whether to continue on and sit down with them or to go someplace else. I turned around and saw Bessie standing back by the door of the church. Reverend Graham was walking my way.

"Cooper," he said as he drew near. "Could I have a word with you?"

I followed him over to the side of the church. I glanced back toward the tables where the adults were sitting. Everyone was silent and looking at the pastor and me.

"Cooper, the folks have heard tell you are attending meetings that the Klan has at Wrightson's Grocery," he said, leaning his head close to mine. "Some also say they saw you in one of the cars the night those mens came and burned down the Harrises' house. If you tell me these things are not true, I'll inform these people that they were mistaken. Is this true or not?"

"I can explain . . ." I said, my voice trembling.

"Just tell me this. Have you been going to the meetings at Wrightson's store?"

"Yes, sir, but . . ."

"And were you in the quarters with the Klansmen when they burned down the Harrises' house?"

"Yes, sir."

Reverend Graham straightened up, and his face seemed twisted in pain. "Cooper, I love you like a son.

We all do. But I am going to have to ask you to leave and never come back to this church."

No one was eating. No one was moving or talking. Everyone was watching me. Bessie was looking toward the parking lot with her back to me.

I turned around and dropped my plate and cup into the five-gallon steel drum trash barrel at the corner of the building and started walking toward Bessie's car. I couldn't stop the tears. Bessie hurried to join me.

As we were driving away, I said to her, "Bessie, it's not fair! You know this is not fair!"

She only shook her head. She was crying too. "I love you, Cooper," she said. "Honest to God I do."

THIRTY-SIX

MISSY WAS ON THE FRONT PORCH playing with her new kitten when I got home. "Get that dumb cat out the way," I said, almost stepping on it as I stormed past and jerked open the screen door.

"I'm gonna tell," she called after me.

I let the door slam behind me as I stepped into the house. Mama and Nana were at the dining-room table, smoking their Winstons. They looked up at me. Poppa was sitting in the front room, watching television.

Mama smiled. "Did you remember to bring back my bowl?" she asked.

"No," I said, hurrying past them.

"No *ma'am*," Poppa corrected without looking around.

I went into my bedroom and snatched off my clip-on tie and threw it on the floor and started taking off my shirt.

Mama came to the doorway. "How was church?" she asked.

"I ain't ever going back," I said.

"What happened?" she asked.

"Nothing!" I said.

"It was an old bowl anyways," she said. "Don't worry about it. I'll talk to Bessie and see about getting it back."

I put on a T-shirt and pair of dungarees and rode my scooter over to Chicago's.

"It ain't fair!" I exclaimed as soon as I walked into the house.

He was lying on a couch, listening to his new classical album. "What?" he said, sitting up.

I told him what had happened. "And Bessie just acted like she didn't know anything about what I'm doing."

"That's because she doesn't," he said. "Neither does Reverend Graham. I thought it best if no one—not them, not the FBI, not anyone but me—knew. Have you had lunch?"

"I'm not hungry."

"I'll make you a peanut butter sandwich. Sit at the table."

He poured a glass of sweet milk and made the sandwich, set them in front of me, then sat down across the table. "This is the hard thing," he said. "We're so isolated, so alone in this."

I sipped my milk. "What do you mean?" I asked.

"It's like this," he said. "This whole movement is to gain Negroes their just and equal rights. So, Negroes who are involved are liable to get beaten up or even killed, but—and this is a very important 'but'—they have the full support of their families and friends, of everyone whose opinion they respect. The same with these young white boys and girls coming down here from the North. They've got everybody at home supporting them and they are heroes to their families and friends. And they know even if they get killed they'll be martyrs, heroes. Do you see what I mean?"

I nodded and chewed. I really wasn't sure I understood anything except I was trying to help by being Gabriel, and the people I was trying to help didn't want anything to do with me.

"On the other hand," he continued, "you and I don't have any of that. By helping, we don't get the respect of those we love. Our families and friends and everyone else we know will probably come to despise us. We have absolutely no support. If we get killed, no one will say what a wonderful hero we were. No one."

"I don't want to be a hero," I said. "I just want my church and friends back."

He reached across the table and put his hand on mine. "You'll get it all back. Just be patient."

"Why can't at least Bessie know? She's just like the others. They think I helped burn down Jubal's house. They think I'm out to hurt them. Why can't we tell Reverend Graham?"

"No," said Uncle Chicago firmly. "We can't take any chances, and right now we need you just where you are. In fact, this may help keep you even safer. When the word gets back to Russell Wrightson and the others—and I'm sure it will—that Oak Grove has kicked you out, they won't be as likely to suspect you are Gabriel." He paused, then said, "This may be one of the best things that could have happened."

"Not as far as I'm concerned."

"Listen. You said Mr. Wrightson is planning something really big, right?"

I nodded.

"We need you in place to find out what it is. That's the only way we can help Bessie and Jubal and the others. Whatever big thing they have in mind is sure to hurt them. Don't you see that?"

"I do," I said reluctantly. "But even Jubal . . . and we were supposed to be 'One for all and all for one.'"

"Sometimes one has to be for all even if the all desert him," he said.

I took a bite of my sandwich. I wanted to understand that. But it didn't make things any easier.

THIRTY-SEVEN

THERE NEVER WAS A TIME in my life that I felt more alone or hurt or bitter than the following week. Jubal and Alvina didn't come to the house at all. Glory came to prepare supper each evening, but she was very cold toward me, only speaking if I first spoke to her.

I didn't go into detail, but I did tell Mama again I really wasn't going to church anymore. Nana told me that she was sure it was all for the best. She loved Bessie to death, she said, but it was time for me to go to a white church if I had a mind to go to church, and she was sure I could go with Missy to First Baptist.

Chicago was the only one who really understood what I was going through. He tried to assure me all this would pass.

There was no called meeting at Wrightson's. Mingled with my grief was a cold, gnawing terror. It was the terror that somehow Mr. Wrightson would find out—or already had found out—that I was the one who got the warning to Johnny Harris.

On Saturday morning Alvina didn't come to art. Bessie came by. She seemed to have aged ten years in the last week. She hadn't been well, she said, and was in bed three days. She seemed so forlorn, crushed. When she finally looked at me, her eyes filled with tears and she hurried out of the house and left in her car.

"She's really hurting," Uncle Chicago said.

"She's hurting!" I said, fighting back my own tears. "I'm the one that's hurting! Couldn't you at least tell Reverend Graham? I can't stand him thinking I'm a traitor."

"We're only doing what we have to do to keep you safe. If Russell Wrightson finds out you're Gabriel, what then? What good will that do the good people at Oak Grove?"

I told Uncle Chicago I couldn't concentrate at all on painting and cleaned my palette and brushes.

I went home to my bedroom and lay down on the bed. I stayed there most of the afternoon. I overheard Nana telling Mama that maybe I was in love. Neither of them had any idea who the girl might be.

I ate little supper and went to bed early. I didn't fall asleep for a long time. I fretted and tossed about. All of life seemed completely unfair.

I'm not sure what time I finally did fall asleep, but I was dead to the world and had a weird dream about walking to school one morning. The tardy bell was ringing and ringing and I was trying to run into the front doors but my legs wouldn't move. My feet felt like they were stuck in concrete, and the bell kept ringing.

I woke up with a start. It was the telephone.

I heard Mama in the hallway. "Hello?"

There was a long pause. Then, "Where? How is he?"

"What's going on?" asked Poppa.

"We'll be right there," said Mama.

She slammed down the receiver and said to Poppa, "That was the sheriff. James has been hurt."

We all scrambled into our clothes and left in the truck with Poppa driving, Mama and Nana sitting in the cab with him, and me and Missy in the back.

Uncle Chicago's car had crashed into a ditch when he was driving from the quarters to the highway. The ambulance was already on the scene when we arrived. He was lying on his back with his eyes closed. His face was a mask of blood, and there was a deep gash in his forehead.

Several people from the quarters, including Reverend Graham, stood in the road. "Sheriff, we got a witness," Reverend Graham said.

"What?" asked Sheriff Skinner. He was watching the attendants slide a large board under Uncle Chicago. Nana had her hands on the sides of his face and was talking to him.

"We got someone who saw the whole thing." Reverend Graham was holding Tommy Clifton by the wrist and pulling him forward. He was an elderly man who lived in a cabin across the road. "Tommy was sitting on his porch and saw a car force Mr. James off the road. Then the men in the car pulled Mr. James out of his car and started beating him up."

Sheriff Skinner stared at Tommy for a moment then said to a deputy, "Take him to my car and wait for me." He watched the attendants place the board with Uncle Chicago onto a gurney and slide it into the ambulance.

"Get in the truck," Poppa said to me.

Nana rode in the ambulance with Uncle Chicago, and Missy and I squeezed into the cab with Mama and Poppa. We raced after the ambulance at seventy miles-an-hour all the way to Tupelo.

At the hospital, we waited outside the emergency room while they worked on Uncle Chicago.

Bessie and Reverend Graham arrived. "Tommy said it was too dark to recognize any of those men," Reverend Graham said.

I looked at Poppa. He was looking away.

After half an hour, the doctor came out. "We're taking him to x-ray," he said. "Both legs are broken, and one arm. He probably has a concussion too, and there are several lacerations to be closed. But he's going to be okay."

"Can I see him?" asked Nana.

"Just for a moment," he said.

After Nana, the rest of us got to go in two at a time. Uncle Chicago's eyes were swollen shut, and his head was bandaged.

Bessie and Reverend Graham left, saying they'd check with us tomorrow. We remained at the hospital several hours. Nana stayed when we finally left for home.

As we were pulling out of the hospital parking lot, Poppa said, "He needs to let this business alone. He don't really understand the kind of people he's messing with."

Mama said, "I don't want to talk about it. I'm too upset."

Missy and I were both asleep when we got home. Poppa carried her into the house and Mama walked beside me with her arm around my shoulders.

THIRTY-EIGHT

WE WERE ALL DRAGGING in the morning at breakfast. Mama's good friend Ida came by for her, and they drove over to Tupelo to the hospital. Mama said that there wasn't any need for all of us to go, that Uncle Chicago wasn't nearly up to receiving visitors, and she wanted us to stay home.

It was Sunday, and I knew Bessie wasn't coming by for me. She had always come by, even when I was sick and couldn't go to church. She came by just to see how I was. But no more.

At the hospital she and Reverend Graham had been friendly to me, but neither said anything about me and church.

I sat in the swing on the front porch and watched the road. I fantasized that Reverend Graham and Bessie had talked on the way back from Tupelo last night, and he told her there had been a mistake, that they knew even if I had been to meetings at Wrightson's store that, after all, I was a baptized church member and should be coming to Oak Grove and nowhere else.

Missy's ride came and she left. I sat another twenty minutes then went down to the pond and sat under a tree and chunked dirt clods into the water for a long time. That night was the revival service at the church with the Memphis preacher, and Bessie wouldn't be coming by for me for that either. I threw a clod as far as I could. The water shot high into the air when the clod broke the surface.

Missy made sandwiches for lunch, and I watched television for a while. I wished Mama had taken me with her. I wanted to see Uncle Chicago.

Poppa went out to the barn a lot more than usual that afternoon. Once he said to me in passing, "There weren't no call for them to do that to Chicago. None at all."

I asked if we could go to Tupelo to see Uncle Chicago. He said, no. This wasn't a good time. "He's going to be all right, though," he said.

I prayed he would.

In the late afternoon I went to the front yard and crawled up into the magnolia tree and sat. Uncle Chicago was right. No one would think either of us was a hero if we died. Probably no one would come to my funeral even. Who would do it? Reverend Graham? Dr. Forhems? They'd probably ask him since he was Missy's pastor and the only white minister connected with the family. But I'd rather have Reverend Graham.

I began to daydream that after I died, Chicago would be out of the hospital and would go to Oak Grove and tell them I was only going to Wrightson's Grocery so I could find out what they were doing and—

A car pulled up into the driveway. A maroon Mercury. It was Casey Donald's car. He parked near the house and got out. Why was he here?

He went up onto the front porch and knocked. Poppa came to the door, stepped outside. They talked for a few minutes. Then Casey left, and Poppa went back inside.

I dropped to the ground and walked into the house, but Poppa was gone. I went out the back door and walked down to the barn. I walked slow to give him time to get his drink before I got there.

"Hey, son," he said merrily as I walked into the barn. He was standing in front of the tool room, holding one hand behind his back. "I was just checking on the dogs."

I stood waiting for him to tell me why Casey Donald had come. Since I'd begun working as Gabriel, there was always a tightness in my chest, but it knotted up a bit more whenever I thought there was the danger I might be found out. Maybe Casey knew.

"There's going to be a meeting at the store tonight," Poppa said.

"And?" My voice was almost choked. I knew exactly that this meeting was about Mr. Wrightson's "something big."

"And we ain't going."

"Ain't going . . . ?" I didn't expect that. "But . . . but, we *have* to."

He gave me a surprised look. "Really? Since when was you so all fired up about going?"

"I mean, well . . . what would they think?"

He seemed to consider about what I meant for a few moments. "Well, all right. I guess we could just go. That doesn't mean we have to do anything." He nodded, then said, "You go on back to the house. I'll be in directly."

The meeting was not until eight o'clock. Darkness had fallen, but the air was still sticky hot. The men and boys came into the storeroom carrying shotguns and rifles. There seemed to be a nervousness in the quiet way everyone was talking. No one knew what to expect.

A cardboard box was in the middle of the floor. A rifle lay across the top of the box.

Mr. Wrightson shook Poppa's hand. "Sorry about Chicago," he said. "I can't imagine anybody doing such a thing."

Poppa didn't answer.

Mr. Wrightson got everyone's attention and thanked them for coming and for coming prepared. As he talked, I counted fourteen men.

"We have a big mission tonight," he said, "and we are going to leave straight from this room and we're all going together. That way we can be assured no warnings will get out to the wrong ears." He paused and grinned. "Everybody ready for some major action?"

Several men nodded. Reno McCarthy said, "Yes, sir!" He had his .22 rifle in his hands. Most of the men just stood waiting to be told why they were there.

Mr. Wrightson bent down and removed the gun from the box. He opened the flaps and reached in with his hand and brought out a dull red stick of dynamite.

"We got a whole box full here," he said. "Tonight that Oak Grove Church is having a meeting. They'll be there a while doing all that jumping and whooping and hollering they call church. And tonight we are going to surround that church and help them all go right straight up to heaven." He gave a big laugh.

No one else laughed except Reno. I had stopped breathing. Was he saying what I thought he was saying? The faces of Bessie and Jubal and Alvina and Glory and Jerome and Reverend Graham all flashed through my mind.

"We're only taking one car and one pickup," he said. "We are going to leave right now. Any questions?"

"Am I hearing you right?" Poppa asked. "You're going to *bomb* that church?"

"That's exactly what we are going to do, Angus," Mr. Wrightson replied. "You have a problem with that?"

"As a matter of fact, I do," Poppa said. "There are children in there. Lots of children."

"Is the poison in a baby rattlesnake deadly?" said

Wrightson. "Just as deadly as that of an adult rattlesnake. These children will grow up to marry your own grandchildren. Is that what you want? Would you let your son here marry one?"

"That's not the point," said Poppa.

"That's exactly the point."

"Well, I ain't going," said Poppa, standing up. "Teaching a few young bucks their place is one thing. Killing children is something else. Come on, Cooper."

"Sit down," said Mr. Wrightson. "Ain't nobody going nowhere until I say so."

"I ain't going either," said Guin Peoney.

Mr. Wrightson looked around the room. "Who else? Any of the rest of you so soft? Any of the rest of you care so little for your wives and daughters that you don't know we're in a war?"

No one said anything.

"Okay," said Mr. Wrightson. He looked at Poppa, then at Guin. "You all don't have to go. I'm not going to make you. But you ain't leaving ahead of us, either. You'll wait until we're good and gone and then you can take your yellow hides home. And I never want to see either one of you again. Ever!"

"But you can't leave them here," said Moses Jackson. "What if they telephone the church?"

Mr. Wrightson smiled and said, "Oak Grove Church ain't got a phone. I've checked. And the only way to the church now that the Bear Creek bridge is out is through the Taylor community. As long as they're here when we leave, they can't get there before we do."

Guin and Poppa and I stood in the parking lot and watched as the others piled into Mr. Wrightson's Oldsmobile and into someone else's GMC pickup.

Then they drove away. Guin got into his car and headed the opposite way, toward his house. Poppa and I followed the red taillights of the Oldsmobile and pickup through town and onto the highway leading to our house.

I was sweating hard and felt chilled at the same time. "But . . . but they can't do this!" I said.

"Believe me, son, if there was any way to stop them I would do it. As fast as they're going, even the sheriff couldn't catch up with them if we was to phone him, even if he was of a mind to go out for something like this on a Sunday night, which I highly doubt. There is just nothing anybody can do."

THIRTY-NINE

POPPA PARKED beside the house. "I'll be in in a bit," he said, moving away toward the barn.

I was now Gabriel but I couldn't get the message to anyone. Bessie and Reverend Graham were inside the church and had no way of knowing about the car and pickup with men and guns and dynamite speeding their way. And Uncle Chicago was in the hospital.

Nowhere to turn. All Poppa really thought about was his bottle.

Bottle? Of course. Gathering bottles with Jubal on Oak Grove Road flashed across my mind like a streak of lightning. How fast could I run a mile? Seven minutes? Amen!

I rushed into the house. Missy and Mama and Nana were watching television with the volume turned up loud like Nana liked it.

I stood in the hallway looking in the phone book. I found the number, lifted the receiver, and dialed. The phone was answered on the first ring.

"Yes?" came a high-pitched voice with a Yankee accent.

"Mr. Shapiro," I said. "It's urgent."

"He's not available. Who is this?"

"Tell him this. Tell him there's going to be big trouble in just a little while at the Oak Grove Baptist Church. He needs to come as fast as possible." I slowly and carefully explained how to take the turnoff to the Taylor community, to turn left on Shubuta Road, and how to reach the church from there. Then I hung up.

There was no way in blazes the FBI would get there in less than an hour. I ran my hand over my mouth. How much time? In twenty minutes the car and pickup would reach the church. With the music and singing and praising the Lord, no one would begin to hear them surrounding the building and placing the sticks of dynamite underneath.

I dashed outside, started my scooter, and bounced down the drive and onto the highway to Oak Grove Road. It was a mile and a half to the washed out bridge at Bear Creek and another mile at least beyond that to the church.

I turned the throttle wide open as I roared down the road. Swarms of bugs swirled into my headlight beam and pounded me in the face. The thought occurred to me that, since my headlight only reached a few yards in front, I might not see the creek in time, might crash into it, but I held the scooter at top speed.

It was only a couple of minutes, but it seemed like

an eternity before I reached the creek. I did cut my speed slightly before I got to it, then braked in the gravel with the rear end sliding almost completely around before I stopped in the dark waist-high shag grass off the shoulder of the road.

I worked my way down the bank in the darkness, hoping I wouldn't step on a snake, and did trip on something once, a limb or root, and sprawled head-long. There was a pain in my right palm. Something had jabbed into it, but I scrambled to my feet immediately and plunged into the black water.

It was only two or three feet deep. I surged to the other bank and crawled up, clawing at grass and bushes as I fought my way up the bank to the road. Then I ran.

Water sloshed in my shoes, and my soaked dunga-rees pulled at me, but I ran as hard as I could, sprint-ing at first then holding the pace that Jubal and I ran in the mornings when we were doing three miles.

I tried to picture how far Mr. Wrightson and the others were. Certainly they had passed through the Taylor community. But had they reached Shubuta Road, the road which led back toward Oak Grove Road? The intersection of Shubuta Road and Oak Grove Road was about three quarters of a mile from the Bear Creek bridge. A narrow dirt road then led from the intersection through a heavy woods and crossed the plank bridge over the stream just before it reached the church house.

I ran harder. Sweat flowed into my eyes, and my lungs heaved and my legs hurt.

I reached the intersection, paused in the middle and looked into the darkness up Shubuta Road and listened. All was quiet. Dead quiet. I didn't even hear a cricket. No glimmer of a headlight.

I rushed on up the narrow road toward the church, passing the swamp on the left, pushing, fearing my legs might crumble at any second, praying, gasping. I could hear the singing and see the lights from the windows of the church before I got to the plank bridge. I stumbled over the bridge, almost falling. The boards were loose, not nailed down.

I looked behind me, thinking I heard the car and the pickup, but I saw no headlights. I ran on to the church, stumbled up the front steps and through the door.

The lights were bright and the people were standing, singing "Amazing Grace." Reverend Graham and the guest minister were on the podium on either side of the pulpit.

I moved down the aisle, my eyes on Reverend Graham, desperately trying to catch a breath. He didn't look my way until I was almost to the front. He stepped off the podium at once and came toward me. The singing slackened and every eye in the congregation was on me and, in that split moment, I realized how strange I must look—fighting to breathe and wet and covered with mud.

Reverend Graham pulled me over to the side by a window. He had his hands on my shoulders and his eyes were wide. "What is it?" he said to me. "Quick. Tell me!"

"They . . . they . . . are coming . . . Mr. Wrightson and . . ."

Reverend Graham let me go and swung around to the congregation and raised both arms into the air to call for complete silence. The piano stopped and every voice was stilled.

"The new Gabriel has brought us a message," he said loudly, his deep voice resounding through the room. "They are coming! Just like we always knew they would. They should be here any minute. Everybody knows what to do. Go! Go! Go!"

There was a scramble of people rushing into the aisles and pouring out through the doors of the church. They were shouting at one another, but there was no confusion. I saw men grabbing up the fire extinguishers and gallons of coal oil. Some of the women were herding the smaller children over to one side of the church.

Bessie rushed up to me and threw her arms around me. "I really knew," she said. "Deep down I knew." She squeezed me so hard she half lifted me from the ground.

Reverend Graham turned back to me and put his arm around my shoulder and squeezed. "I'm sorry things got like they did," he said. "We just didn't know what to think. Then your uncle talked to me last night and told me what you were doing. He was coming from my house when he got jumped." He gave me another squeeze. "Believe me, Cooper, I've been miserable about this all week myself." He glanced back at the doorway and the people running around. "Now, I've got work to do." He moved away and took the arm of Auntie Caroline who, at 103, was the oldest member of the church, and said, "You stay in here, precious, and rest yourself."

"Humph," she said to him, smacking her gums, "I ain't missing this! No sirree!"

I was breathing easier and stepped toward the aisle. Jubal was standing to the side, grinning at me, and Alvina was slightly behind him. She was staring at me with her eyes big as washers and her mouth hanging wide open. "Come on," Jubal said. "We got work to do. Or you gonna be lazy bones as usual?" He laughed and pulled me after him.

"Listen," I said. "Ike Montgomery didn't have anything to do with Marcellus's death."

"I know," he said. "Bessie told me."

The older women, who were clustered around the doorway, smiled at me as we passed. One grabbed me and kissed me on the cheek.

Outside, flashlights were swarming like giant lightning bugs around the plank bridge. I could hear the pastor saying, "Hurry! Hurry!"

I trotted after Jubal.

At the bridge, men were lifting up the loose boards and heaving them to the side of the bank. Other men were pouring out the coal oil in a wide circle around the bridge. Several women were stretching out a long heavy wire and tying it taut on either end to stakes that had already been pounded into the ground.

I saw men standing behind the wire, holding the fire extinguishers, and women holding lengths of rope and flour sacks.

"Listen!" someone screamed. "Listen!"

Everyone grew silent. There was the distinct hum of vehicles. Drawing closer, ever closer.

"Done!" shouted a man with a coal-oil can. All the planks had been removed as well, leaving only the two beams spanning the stream.

All the flashlights were extinguished, and everyone faded back into the darkness. Alvina was standing on one side of me and Jubal on the other.

The sounds of the car and the pickup were very close now. We could hear them slowing on Shubuta Road and making the turn up the narrow road leading to the church. In a moment I saw the headlights through the trees, flickering and bouncing, then straight ahead and they surged on toward us.

The Oldsmobile was in front. It never braked until it was only a few yards from the bridge, then it swerved to the right and plunged over the bank.

The GMC pickup was right behind and shot

straight onto one of the beams and rolled over sideways. The men in the back of the truck flew through the air and crashed down onto the grass and into the stream.

Not far from me a cigarette lighter clicked, and the flame was lowered to the ground. Fire in the coal-oil-soaked grass immediately shot up high and crackled and roared as it swept around on both sides, completely encircling the car and truck.

I could hear somebody groaning and then the men inside the ring of fire beginning to yell. "Help us! Help us!" came a cry.

"Oh, God, save us!" screamed someone else.

"The dynamite! The dynamite! It's going to go."

"Throw out your guns!" roared Reverend Graham's voice. "Now!"

Through the flames came several rifles and shotguns and pistols.

"Hurry up!" shouted Reverend Graham. "Every single one!"

Another rifle tore through the fire and landed in the grass in front of me.

The men with fire extinguishers stepped forward and blasted a small four-foot-wide area of the fire circle then quickly stepped back. They had made a single gap in the flames.

A moment later one of the Klansmen darted out through the gap, tripped over the wire, and plunged into the weeds. He was set upon at once by men and women with ropes. They snatched his hands behind his back and tied them together then yanked a flour sack over his head.

Two more darted out, tripped, and were set upon. Then several, one behind the other, all screaming, and all tripped and were grabbed at once.

After a while, no more came out. Nine men lay on the ground groaning, tied and flour-sacked. I heard the muffled but unmistakable voice of Reno McCarthy coming from behind one of the sacks. He was sobbing. "Please don't hurt me," he whimpered. "Please have mercy."

Reverend Graham stepped beside me. "We have nine," he said.

"There were eleven in all," I said. Fourteen of us had been in the room, counting Guin Peoney, Poppa, and me.

"Two must still be in there," he said. Then he signaled the men with fire extinguishers to put out the fire. "But be careful. We still have two unaccounted for."

The flames were snuffed out quickly and flashlights at once beamed onto the two vehicles. The Oldsmobile had nosed over the bank and into the stream. The pickup was on its side also in the stream.

"Here's one!" someone on the other side shouted.

"Got another one here!" I recognized Jerome's voice.

The man on the other bank was Casey Donald. He

was groaning and just regaining consciousness. The other man was sitting on the ground. It was Mr. Wrightson. He too was stunned. Both were quickly tied up and flour-sacked.

The Klansmen, hooded with the white flour sacks and unable to see, were pulled to their feet and herded together. Women poked broom handles at them, which the Klansmen obviously thought were guns. In a few minutes, both Casey and Mr. Wrightson were brought to join the others.

"Now," said Reverend Graham. "Take them down to the swamp. Y'all know what to do."

All of the Klansmen began groaning and moaning and begging. "No! Please, please, please!" I heard Moses Jackson saying. "You can't kill us! Oh, God! Please!"

"Shut up!" Jerome ordered, prodding him with a broom handle.

Jubal began hissing loudly. And I joined him. Alvina looked at us like we were crazy.

Jerome and the other men were obviously enjoying themselves immensely as they force-marched the Klansmen back down the road in the direction of the swamp. Several women with flashlights searched through the grasses, gathering up the weapons.

Bessie came up and gave me another hug. She noticed the concerned look on my face as I watched the men with flashlights and broom handles walking the Klansman down the road.

She chuckled. "They are just going to turn them loose in the swamp and let the mosquitoes play with them for the night," she said.

Tamara Feinstein and Esther Garrison both gave me hugs, too. "I can't imagine anyone being so brave," Tamara said.

"He's pretty handsome too," said Esther, winking at me.

Jubal grinned and laughed and put his hands on my head and shook it back and forth. "You are one crazy man!" he said.

"I just wish Squirrel could be here," I said.

Alvina, her hands on her hips, stepped up to me. "Not too shabby," she said with an almost smile. "For a white boy."

"Thank you, Fly," I said, grinning at her.

The FBI agents in two cars and a van didn't arrive for over two hours. In spite of my good directions, they'd made some wrong turns. They found most of the Klansmen on the edge of the swamp, stumbling around, terrified. The rest were found in the morning.

All were arrested and charged with conspiracy to violate the civil rights of the church members. None was ever convicted of anything, but neither did they meet at Wrightson's Grocery anymore or cause any more trouble. And none of them ever figured out how the congregation at the Oak Grove Baptist Church knew they were coming.

FORTY

UNCLE CHICAGO was in the hospital for three weeks. Nana stayed with him at his house two months, until he could take care of himself.

A deer hunter found Ike Montgomery's badly decomposed body in a swamp several miles west of town in the fall. When his will was read, it turned out that Ike left all his properties and possessions to be divided equally. The will read, "between my two nephews, Johnny Harris and Jubal Harris, and my niece, Alvina Harris."

Jubal, in spite of the recently enacted state law allowing freedom of choice, elected to return to Washington High, where he started at tackle on the football team until the beginning of his junior year, when court-ordered total desegregation turned Washington into a junior high school for both whites and blacks and forced Jubal to attend Chulosa High School his last two years. He starred in athletics and, after graduating, went to the University of Mississippi on a football scholarship.

At the end of that summer, Alvina chose to enroll at the previously all white Colbert Junior High, my school, for the fall semester. She went on to Chulosa High all four years where she was a cheerleader each year and was vice president of the student council her senior year. She then enrolled at the University of California at Berkeley.

During my senior year in high school, I received a postcard from Squirrel. It was postmarked Santa Fe, New Mexico, and on the back was a photograph of a scorpion. The note read, "Thought you might want to hang this up in the Lair. Squirrel." There was no return address.

Jubal and I, I should mention, had made the cabin his daddy grew up in our new Scorpion meeting place. We rarely returned to our original clubhouse.

After high school, with the guidance of Uncle Chicago, I entered his alma mater, the Art Institute of Chicago. And frequently while I was there, on cold wintry days, I walked along the water's edge at the 31st Street beach and looked out onto fog-blanketed Lake Michigan and thought about a long hot summer and a church called Oak Grove and the angel Gabriel and how he made me free forever.

JOHN ARMISTEAD is an ordained minister, artist, and religion journalist, and formerly taught kindergarten and high school. In addition to his novel, *The $66 Summer,* which won the 2000 Milkweed Prize for Children's Literature, he has published *A Legacy of Vengeance, A Homecoming for Murder,* and *Cruel As the Grave.* He lives with his wife, Sandi, in Tupelo, Mississippi, where he tries to divide his time equitably between painting, riding his Harley-Davidson, and his three grandchildren.

IF YOU ENJOYED THIS BOOK, YOU'LL ALSO WANT TO READ THESE OTHER MILKWEED NOVELS.

To order books or for more information, contact Milkweed at (800) 520-6455 or visit our website (www.milkweed.org).

THE $66 SUMMER
by John Armistead

MILKWEED PRIZE FOR CHILDREN'S LITERATURE
NEW YORK PUBLIC LIBRARY BEST BOOKS OF THE YEAR: "BOOKS FOR THE TEEN AGE"

By working at his grandmother's general store in Obadiah, Alabama, during the summer of 1955, George Harrington figures he can save enough money to buy the motorcycle he wants, a Harley-Davidson. Spending his off-hours with two friends, Esther Garrison, fourteen, and Esther's younger brother, Bennett, the unusual trio in 1950s Alabama—George is white and Esther and Bennett are black—embark on a summer of adventure that turns serious when they begin to uncover the truth about the racism in their midst.

GILDAEN, THE HEROIC ADVENTURES OF A MOST UNUSUAL RABBIT
by Emilie Buchwald

CHICAGO TRIBUNE BOOK FESTIVAL AWARD, BEST BOOK FOR AGES 9–12

Gildaen is befriended by a mysterious being who has lost his memory but not the ability to change shape at will. Together they accept the perilous task of thwarting the evil sorcerer, Grimald, in this tale of magic, villainy, and heroism.

THE OCEAN WITHIN
by V. M. Caldwell

MILKWEED PRIZE FOR CHILDREN'S LITERATURE

Elizabeth is a foster child who has just been placed with the boisterous and affectionate Sheridans, a family that wants to adopt her. Accustomed to having to fend for herself, however, Elizabeth is reluctant to open up to them. During a summer spent by the ocean with the eight Sheridan children and their grandmother, dubbed by Elizabeth as "Iron Woman" because of her strict discipline, Elizabeth learns what it means—and how much she must risk—to become a permanent member of a loving family.

TIDES
by V. M. Caldwell

Recently adopted twelve-year-old Elizabeth Sheridan is looking forward to spending the summer at Grandma's oceanside home. But on her stay there, she faces problems involving her cousins, five-year-old Petey and eighteen-year-old Adam, that cause her to question whether the family will hold together. As she and Grandma help each other through troubling times, Elizabeth comes to see that she has become an important member of the family.

PARENTS WANTED
by George Harrar

MILKWEED PRIZE FOR CHILDREN'S LITERATURE

After five "adoption parties" and no luck, Andy Fleck, the kid nobody wanted, faces his biggest challenge yet—learning how to live with parents who seem to love him. Placed in a new foster home with Jeff and Laurie, he has a chance to get out of the grip of his past, which includes a jailed father and a mother who gave him up to the state. But Andy can't keep himself from challenging every limit that his foster parents set. So far, Laurie and Jeff have refused to give up on their difficult new charge. But will he go too far?

No Place
by Kay Haugaard

Arturo Morales and his fellow sixth-grade classmates decide to improve their neighborhood and their lives by building a park in their otherwise concrete, inner-city Los Angeles barrio. The kids are challenged by their teachers to figure out what it would take to transform the neighborhood junkyard into a clean, safe place for children to play. Despite their parents' skepticism and the threat of street gangs, Arturo and his classmates struggle to prove that the actions of individuals—even kids—can make a difference.

The Monkey Thief
by Aileen Kilgore Henderson

NEW YORK PUBLIC LIBRARY BEST BOOKS OF THE YEAR: "BOOKS FOR THE TEEN AGE"

Twelve-year-old Steve Hanson is sent to Costa Rica for eight months to live with his uncle. There he discovers a world completely unlike anything he can see from the cushions of his couch back home, a world filled with giant trees and insects, mysterious sounds, and the constant companionship of monkeys swinging in the branches overhead. When Steve hatches a plan to capture a monkey for himself, his quest for a pet leads him into dangerous territory. It takes all of Steve's survival skills—and the help of his new friends—to get him out of trouble.

THE SUMMER OF THE BONEPILE MONSTER
by Aileen Kilgore Henderson

MILKWEED PRIZE FOR CHILDREN'S LITERATURE
ALABAMA LIBRARY ASSOCIATION 1996 JUVENILE/YOUNG ADULT AWARD
MAUDE HART LOVELACE AWARD FINALIST

Eleven-year-old Hollis Orr has been sent to spend the summer with Grancy, his father's grandmother, in rural Dolliver, Alabama, while his parents "work things out." As summer begins, Hollis encounters a road called Bonepile Hollow, barred by a gate and a real skull and crossbones mounted on a board. "Things that go down that road don't ever come back," he is told. Thus begins the mystery that plunges Hollis into real danger.

TREASURE OF PANTHER PEAK
by Aileen Kilgore Henderson

NEW YORK PUBLIC LIBRARY BEST BOOKS OF THE YEAR: "BOOKS FOR THE TEEN AGE"

Twelve-year-old Page Williams begrudgingly accompanies her mother, Ellie, as she flees her abusive husband, Page's father. Together they settle in a fantastic new world—Big Bend National Park, Texas. Wild animals stalk through the park, and the nearby Ghost Mountains are filled with legends of lost treasures. As Page tests her limits by sneaking into forbidden canyons, Ellie struggles to win the trust of other parents. Only through their newfound courage are they able to discover a treasure beyond what they could have imagined.

I Am Lavina Cumming
by Susan Lowell

MOUNTAINS & PLAINS BOOKSELLERS ASSOCIATION AWARD

In 1905, ten-year-old Lavina is sent from her home on the Bosque Ranch in Arizona Territory to live with her aunt in the city of Santa Cruz, California. Armed with the Cumming family motto, "courage," Lavina deals with a new school, homesickness, a very spoiled cousin, an earthquake, and a big decision about her future.

The Boy with Paper Wings
by Susan Lowell

Confined to bed with a viral fever, eleven-year-old Paul sails a paper airplane into his closet and propels himself into mysterious and dangerous realms in this exciting and fantastical adventure. Paul finds himself trapped in the military diorama on his closet floor, out to stop the evil commander, KRON. Armed only with paper and the knowledge of how to fold it, Paul uses his imagination and courage to find his way out of dilemmas and disasters.

The Secret of the Ruby Ring
by Yvonne MacGrory

WINNER OF IRELAND'S BISTO "BOOK OF THE YEAR" AWARD

Lucy gets a very special birthday present, a star ruby ring, from her grandmother and finds herself transported to Langley Castle in the Ireland of 1885. At first, she is intrigued by castle life, in which she is the lowliest servant, until she loses the ruby ring and her only way home.

EMMA AND THE RUBY RING
by Yvonne MacGrory

Only one day short of her eleventh birthday and looking forward to spending time with her dad, Emma wakes up not at her cousin Lucy's, where she has been visiting, but in a nineteenth-century Irish workhouse. Emma learns that the ruby ring can grant two wishes to its wearer, and now, at a time of dire historical unrest, she must prove she can be the heroic girl she wants to be.

A BRIDE FOR ANNA'S PAPA
by Isabel R. Marvin

MILKWEED PRIZE FOR CHILDREN'S LITERATURE

Life on Minnesota's iron range in 1907 is not easy for thirteen-year-old Anna Kallio. Her mother's death has left Anna to take care of the house, her young brother, and her father, a blacksmith in the dangerous iron mines. So she and her brother plot to find their father a new wife, even attempting to arrange a match with one of the "mail order" brides arriving from Finland.

MINNIE
by Annie M. G. Schmidt

WINNER OF THE NETHERLANDS' SILVER PENCIL PRIZE AS ONE OF THE BEST BOOKS OF THE YEAR

Miss Minnie is a cat. Or rather, she *was* a cat. She is now a human, and she's not at all happy to be one. As Minnie tries to find and reverse the cause of her transformation, she brings her reporter friend, Mr. Tibbs, news from the cats' gossip hotline—including revealing information that one of the town's most prominent citizens is not the animal lover he appears to be.

THE DOG WITH GOLDEN EYES
by Frances Wilbur

Many girls dream of owning a dog of their own, but Cassie's wish for one takes an unexpected turn in this contemporary tale of friendship and growing up. Thirteen-year-old Cassie is lonely, bored, and feeling friendless when a large, beautiful dog appears one day in her suburban backyard. Cassie wants to adopt the dog, but as she learns more about him, she realizes that she is, in fact, caring for a full-grown Arctic wolf. As she attempts to protect the wolf from urban dangers, Cassie discovers that she possesses strengths and resources she never imagined.

BEHIND THE BEDROOM WALL
by Laura E. Williams

It is 1942. Thirteen-year-old Korinna Rehme is an active member of her local *Jungmädel,* a Nazi youth group, along with many of her friends. Korinna's parents, however, secretly are members of an underground group providing a means of escape to the Jews of their city and are, in fact, hiding a refugee family behind the wall of Korinna's bedroom. As Korinna comes to know the family, especially their young daughter, her sympathies begin to turn. But when someone tips off the Gestapo, loyalties are put to the test and Korinna must decide in what she believes and whom she trusts.

THE SPIDER'S WEB
by Laura E. Williams

Thirteen-year-old Lexi Jordan has just joined the Pack, a group of neo-Nazi skinheads, as a substitute for the close-knit family she wishes she had. After she and the Pack spray paint a synagogue, Lexi hides from her pursuers on the front porch of elderly Ursula Zeidler's home, a former member of the Hitler Youth Group, who painfully recalls her ugly anti-Semitic Nazi activities and betrayal of a friend. When her younger sister becomes enthralled with Lexi's new "family," Lexi realizes the true meaning of the Pack and has little time to save herself and her sister from its sinister grip.

MILKWEED EDITIONS publishes with the intention of making a humane impact on society, in the belief that literature is a transformative art uniquely able to convey the essential experiences of the human heart and spirit. To that end, Milkweed publishes distinctive voices of literary merit in handsomely designed, visually dynamic books, exploring the ethical, cultural, and esthetic issues that free societies need continually to address. Milkweed Editions is a not-for-profit press.

JOIN US

Since its genesis as *Milkweed Chronicle* in 1979, Milkweed has helped hundreds of emerging writers reach their readers. Thanks to the generosity of foundations and of individuals like you, Milkweed Editions is able to continue its nonprofit mission of publishing books chosen on the basis of literary merit—of how they impact the human heart and spirit—rather than on how they impact the bottom line. That's a miracle that our readers have made possible.

In addition to purchasing Milkweed books, you can join the growing community of Milkweed supporters. Individual contributions of any amount are both meaningful and welcome. Contact us for a Milkweed catalog or log on to www.milkweed.org and click on "About Milkweed," then "Why Join Milkweed," to find out about our donor program, or simply call (800) 520-6455 and ask about becoming one of Milkweed's contributors. As a nonprofit press, Milkweed belongs to you, the community. Milkweed's board, its staff, and especially the authors whose careers you help launch thank you for reading our books and supporting our mission in any way you can.

Interior design by Dale Cooney
Typeset in Plantin 11/15
by Stanton Publication Services, Inc.
Printed on acid-free 55# Sebago 2000 Antique paper
by Maple-Vail Book Manufacturing